CRACKED POT

THE CRACKED POT

MELISSA GLAZER

WHEELER
CHIVERS

This Large Print edition is published by Wheeler Publishing, Waterville, Maine, USA and by BBC Audiobooks Ltd, Bath, England.
Wheeler Publishing, a part of Gale, Cengage Learning.
Copyright © 2008 by The Berkley Publishing Group.
The moral right of the author has been asserted.
A Clay and Crime Mystery.

The text of this Large Print edition is unabridged.
Other aspects of the book may vary from the original edition.
Set in 16 pt. Plantin.
Printed on permanent paper.

LIBRARY OF CONGRESS CATALOGING-IN-PUBLICATION DATA

Glazer, Melissa.
  The cracked pot / by Melissa Glazer.
    p. cm. — (A clay and crime mystery) (Wheeler Publishing large print cozy mystery)
    ISBN-13: 978-1-59722-827-5 (pbk. : alk. paper)
    ISBN-10: 1-59722-827-3 (pbk. : alk. paper)
    1. Pottery—Fiction. 2. Potters—Fiction. 3. Vermont—Fiction. 4. Large type books. I. Title.
  PS3607.L394C73 2008
  813'.6—dc22
                                                    2008028068

BRITISH LIBRARY CATALOGUING-IN-PUBLICATION DATA AVAILABLE

Published in 2008 in the U.S. by arrangement with The Berkley Publishing Group a member of Penguin Group (USA) Inc.
Published in 2009 in the U.K. by arrangement with The Berkley Publishing Group a member of Penguin Group (USA) Inc.

U.K. Hardcover: 978 1 408 42125 3 (Chivers Large Print)
U.K. Softcover: 978 1 408 42126 0 (Camden Large Print)

Printed in the United States of America
1 2 3 4 5 6 7 12 11 10 09 08

For my agent, John Talbot.
"Thanks for everything."

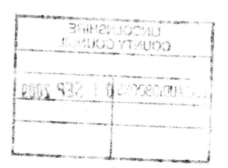

CHAPTER 1

I've lost a great many things in my life, including my temper, my car keys, my mind, and — a long, long time ago — my virginity, but I'd never lost an entire person before Charles Potter came into my life. Or didn't. I know it sounds confusing, but the truth sometimes is.

Let me assure you, there are some things that are certain in my life. My name is Carolyn Emerson, and I run a paint-your-own pottery shop called Fire at Will in the quaint little town of Maple Ridge, Vermont. I've been married to the same man for nearly thirty years, I've got a great assistant, a nearly perfect best friend, and a group of potters known as the Firing Squad who are always there when I need them. And before it became clear exactly how and why the man who called himself Charles Potter disappeared, I would have to lean on every last one of them.

■ ■ ■ ■

"Is he here yet?" my assistant David asked breathlessly as he rushed into Fire at Will. Barely into his twenties, David was a nice-looking young man who just happened to have a long blond ponytail that was still hard for me to get used to seeing on a guy. Tall and a little on the skinny side, David had fingers that any potter would covet, long and slim with a strength to tame the wildest clay. "I didn't miss him, did I?"

"Honestly, David, he's not a rock star. He's a potter, just like you are."

"Come on," David said, "he's Charles Potter. That man can do things with clay I can only dream about."

"I know, I know, he's your hero, but to be honest with you, he didn't sound like a hero when I talked to him yesterday. He was kind of scatterbrained." At David's urging, I'd called Mr. Potter and asked him to come by the shop before his presentation at Travers College, the small liberal arts school on the edge of town. To my surprise, he'd agreed. He was giving a lecture and demonstration at Travers later that night, but he said he'd be delighted to come by Fire at Will on the way. I glanced at the clock and saw that he was now a half hour late. David had gone to the bank for me earlier, albeit reluctantly, and now, waiting on the potter's appearance, he was panting like a dog after a steak.

"I'm not entirely certain he's even going to show up," I said. "Maybe he forgot about us."

My accusation didn't faze David for a second. "He plays by his own set of rules. The man's a genius."

"I've never met a genius before, but if this is the way one acts, I haven't been missing anything. What time is he scheduled to talk at the college?"

David looked at his watch. "He should be starting in less than an hour. I hope nothing's happened to him."

"Don't be so dramatic. What you should really hope is that he remembered at least one of the appearances he agreed to make today." I'd had enough hero worship to last me a month.

"If he misses it, I know he'll have a good reason," David said, already making excuses.

"Is Annie going to the demonstration with you?" Annie Gregg was David's first serious girlfriend. The relationship had begun because of Annie's remarkable resemblance to Julia Roberts, the lovely and talented actress — and David's other infatuation. Annie was cleaning houses to save up for

Stanford, and David often complained that she spent more time amassing her tuition than she did with him.

"She's busy cleaning a house, but as soon as she finishes, she's going to meet me there."

"Maybe you should go on to the school," I suggested. "You wouldn't want to get a bad seat for the demonstration." Or stay here and keep driving me crazy, I added to myself.

"Don't worry about that. I've got two seats reserved in the front row."

"You don't have Hannah holding them, do you? Your mother has better things to do than sit in an auditorium all day saving you seats." Hannah was David's mother and also my best friend, an arrangement that sometimes led to complications but was generally a good thing for all concerned. She was also an English professor at the college and the push behind David getting a formal education there.

"Are you kidding me? She thinks I'm crazier than you do. I paid Kelly Winston to do it. In exchange for reserving two seats for me, I'm giving her a free lesson in throwing a bowl on the wheel. You don't mind, do you?"

"Why should I mind? It's just my business

10

and the way I earn my living. If you want to give my money away, what right do I have to object?" When I looked at his face, I saw that I'd gone a little too far with my teasing, something I had a habit of doing with young David. "Relax, I'm kidding. Of course I don't mind."

"Thanks, Carolyn." He glanced at his watch again. "Maybe I should call the hospital, or even the sheriff. He'd know if Mr. Potter had been in an accident, wouldn't he?"

"I doubt Sheriff Hodges would know if he had hit the man with his own patrol car." John Hodges was our sheriff, an older man who was hanging on until he could retire with full benefits. Many townspeople thought he was a little less than diligent performing his duties, and I was ready to admit that I was one of the first to come to that conclusion.

David waited at Fire at Will as long as he could. After glancing at the Dali-like melted wall clock for the sixtieth time in twelve minutes, he said reluctantly, "He's not coming, is he?"

"It doesn't look like it." The man had some nerve, agreeing to come by one day and completely blowing me off the next, without so much as a telephone call or an explanation.

David sighed, and as he left the shop, he said, "Promise me you'll get his autograph for me if he comes by here first." He thrust Charles Potter's book, *A Study in Clay,* at me. "Have him personalize it, too."

"Shouldn't you take this with you? It will mean a lot more to you if you see him sign it yourself."

David grinned. "Don't worry about that. I've got another copy out in my car."

"Why am I not surprised." I turned the cover over to get a look at the author, but the back held only a blurb from another author. "What, no photograph?"

"He won't allow pictures of any sort to be taken of him," David explained. "In fact, this is his first public appearance, and I mean ever."

"Then how did he get so well known?"

David shrugged. "He's sold his work through galleries, and he has a presence online. This is his first book, though. There are all kinds of articles about his techniques on the Internet. You really should get a computer, Carolyn."

"What on earth would I possibly use it for? I'm fine with my portable typewriter."

He shook his head. "There's a whole world out there waiting for you."

"Then it'll just have to continue waiting." I wasn't in any mood to be lectured by my assistant on the modern age and the joys of technology. "Hadn't you better go?"

"You're right. Bye, Carolyn."

"Good-bye, David. Have fun, and don't forget to curtsey when you meet him."

"Don't be ridiculous," he said.

"Oh, that's right, boys don't curtsey; they bow."

He rolled his eyes at me much as my own two sons had done once upon a time, and I felt a stab of nostalgia for when they were younger.

After David had gone, I had the shop to myself for the last half hour of my regular business hours, though I wasn't finished with my workday by any means. Tonight, the Firing Squad was meeting, and it was my turn to provide the snacks. Jenna Blake, a retired judge, had instituted a practice where we took turns bringing refreshments to our meetings, since I couldn't afford to feed them without charging more. I contributed whenever it was my turn, and I didn't hesitate to sample what they brought in. It made me feel like a member of the squad instead of its sponsor. Tonight I was hurrying home to make my famous not so Swedish meatballs, and if I knew my husband,

Bill, he would be hovering just underfoot, complaining about being hungry as he ate more than his share of the treats.

"How much is this costing you?" Bill said later that evening at home as I was preparing the night's fare. "Are you going to actually make any money tonight?"

"I'm doing fine; you don't have to worry about my bottom line. This is a goodwill gesture for my group."

"That's all well and good, but don't forget about your husband," he said as he polished off another meatball and picked up one more. "I need some goodwill, too."

"I'm sorry, what did you just say? I couldn't understand you with all that food in your mouth."

He pouted when I said that, something my dear husband was inclined to do, so I quickly added, "Eat all you want. I made a double batch, so there's plenty."

Out of sheer cussedness, he put the toothpick-skewered ball he was holding back on the platter I was filling. "I wouldn't want to deprive your guests."

"Fine, if there are any left, I'll try to remember to bring them back home."

He looked at the meatballs another few seconds, then said, "Knowing you, you'll probably forget. I'd better get my share right now."

"Suit yourself," I said as I turned my back on him. A minute or so later I looked toward him again and saw several more empty toothpicks on his plate. At least I knew Bill wouldn't go hungry tonight. I covered the platter, then leaned over and kissed his cheek. "Don't wait up. We're trying a new technique of weaving clay tonight, and it might take us a while to get it right."

Bill pointed a toothpick at me. "Have you ever done anything like it yourself?"

"No," I admitted reluctantly, "but it looks easy enough."

He shook his head, so I asked, "What?"

"I'm not saying a word."

"You don't have to. I'm perfectly capable of learning how to do something from a book."

I was expecting some kind of retort, not the grin he gave me. "Why are you smiling?"

"Was I? Sorry, didn't mean to."

"Sometimes I'd like to trade you in for a hat."

"You hate hats," he said, still grinning.

"Then I'd give it away, too, and be done with you."

"Come here, woman." He wrapped me in

his arms, and I tingled at his touch; even after all our years together he still made me feel that way. As I gazed up at him, a gooey and romantic expression on my face, he leaned down and whispered in my ear, "Don't forget to bring home the leftovers."

I broke away, smiling despite his less than seductive comment. "Don't worry, I've never forgotten yet, have I?"

When I got to the shop, Sandy Crenshaw — a reference librarian and a charter member of the Firing Squad — was standing out front. Sandy was a cute and curvy young brunette with sparkling brown eyes and a sunny smile.

"Have you been waiting long?" I asked as I tried to get my keys out of my purse while balancing the platter of meatballs in the other hand.

"Here, let me help you with those," she said as she took them from me. "Sorry I'm so early."

"Nonsense," I said as I opened the door to the shop and held it for her. "I could use a hand setting up." I flipped on the lights as I walked inside. The front part of Fire at Will was devoted to folks who wanted to paint their own pottery pieces. There were tables and chairs set up, and along the perimeter were shelves stacked with bisque-fired pottery ready for paint and glaze. The front display window had pieces for sale, along with a table by the cash register for more items. I was amazed at how many of the pieces I sold were already finished. Not that I minded, but I much preferred folks to come in and actually paint or work with the raw clay themselves. Behind the paint studio, in the back, were the potter's wheels and the worktables for shaping raw clay. I had as many customers who liked hand-building as I did those who liked throwing on one of our wheels. Behind that was my office, a bathroom, and a storage area. Fire at Will didn't have a big footprint, but I'd managed to cram a lot of activity into it.

"What would you like me to do?" Sandy asked as she put the meatballs down on our snack table.

"You could get out the hot plate so we can keep those warm," I said.

As she did that, I started laying out some of the tools we'd need tonight. There were five of us in the Firing Squad. I never counted David, since he usually had night classes at Travers. He had brokered a deal with his mother early on. If he could work at Fire at Will during the day creating the pottery he loved, he would attend night classes at Travers for her benefit. Hannah had reluctantly agreed, so whenever the two of them had a conflict, I always managed to get stuck squarely in the middle of it.

After arranging the tools for the evening's activities, I cut off five chunks of clay from one of the bags I stored in a broken refrigerator and started kneading them. It would save some time if I had the clay ready when the others arrived.

"Can I help you with that?" Sandy asked.

"Sure, that would be great."

As she took a slab of clay and started working it on the board, she said, "I'm really excited about this."

"Then you need to get out more," I said as I worked out a particularly stubborn air bubble. "How's your love life? Are you still seeing Jake?"

"No, that kind of fizzled out," she admitted.

"Not your one true love?"

Sandy laughed. "Not even in my top ten. To be honest with you, he found someone else."

"Oh, Sandy, I'm so sorry."

"Don't be," she said. "I kind of set it up myself."

I stopped kneading for a second and stared at her. "You're not going to get away with just telling me that much. I want details."

"I had a friend I thought would be better suited for him than I was, so I planned a double date with Jennifer, and I promised to introduce her to a great guy."

"Okay, I'm with you so far."

She grinned, then said, "I got an emergency phone call when we were standing in line at the theater. I had to leave, they went to the movie without me, and now everyone's happier."

"What happened to her blind date?"

"Now why on earth would I go to the trouble of fixing her up with somebody else when I had a perfectly good plan in place to get them together. Jake really is a great guy. He's just not the one for me."

"I don't know how you keep up with it all," I said, laughing. I started thinking about eligible young men I knew who might be right for Sandy. I'd have to do any matchmaking surreptitiously, though. I'd promised Bill years ago that I'd stop meddling in other people's lives, and I always tried to keep my oaths. Most of the time. Okay, I wasn't great at it, but why couldn't he admit that sometimes people needed a little nudge in the right direction, and if I could provide it, didn't I owe that much to my friends? Why shouldn't they be happy, too?

I heard a knock at the front door, so I left the clay at the table and went to the front of the shop. Jenna Blake, the retired judge, along with Butch Hardcastle, the reformed crook, were standing outside. Butch looked like a thug at first glance, big and burly with an intimidating countenance, but he was a teddy bear inside. At least he was with us. Jenna managed to look dignified no matter what the circumstances. She had allowed the gray creeping gently into her hair to remain, and she absolutely exuded power and confidence.

I opened the door for them and stepped aside. "Come on in. Have either one of you spoken with Martha today?" Martha Knotts was the final member of the Firing Squad, a young mother of five who somehow managed to stay reed thin, a quality I had to work not to hate her for.

"She can't make it," Jenna said as I locked the door behind her. "Angie has the flu, and it looks like the others may be coming down with it as well. She sounded rather harried when I spoke with her earlier."

I couldn't imagine that crew of hers all getting sick at the same time. "Is there anything we can do to help?"

"No, she said her mother-in-law was coming to pitch in. The poor girl."

"Don't feel sorry for her," I said. "Martha told me the woman is an absolute dream."

Butch said, "You two can stand here and talk all night, but I want to get started."

"You're impatient tonight," Jenna said.

"Sorry. I've just got an appointment a little later on, and I want to be sure I don't miss it." I wondered at times just how reformed Butch really was, but I was afraid to press him too much about it.

On the other hand, Jenna was not. "Butch Hardcastle, I can't imagine any appointment that late being legitimate."

He grinned at her. "Then you don't have enough imagination, Judge."

"It's Jenna, and you know it. Now stop changing the subject. What possible reason could you have for a business appointment so late in the evening?"

"Who said it was business?" Butch asked, grinning.

Jenna looked embarrassed. "I'm sorry, of course it's none of my business. Your affairs are your own."

Could the oaf not see that the judge was just as interested in him as he was in her? These two were going to need a nudge if they didn't figure it out soon. Foolishness

21

in love wasn't strictly a problem just for young people.

It finally occurred to Butch what Jenna was saying. He frowned as he explained, "It's not a date, if that's what you're thinking."

Jenna said stiffly, "It's none of my concern, even if it is."

"But I just said it wasn't."

They weren't getting anywhere on their own. I was about to say something to help when Sandy came through. "Aren't you coming back? The clay's ready."

"So am I," Butch said as he brushed past us.

Jenna looked at me and said, "Men," putting enough into it to supply a thousand gradients of meaning.

"They're not perfect, but they usually do their best."

"How sad for them," Jenna said. She was in a bit of a sour mood, so I decided not to press her further.

When we were all gathered in back, I suggested, "Why don't we get started, and when we get hungry, we can all take a break."

No one dissented, and we all took up our places at the table. "We're going to weave some clay tonight. First we have to get our balls into flat sheets. Sandy and I have already kneaded these, so they're ready to go. Take your dowels and roll the clay out until it's about a quarter of an inch thick."

They did as I directed, and we soon had our balls converted into sheets of equal thicknesses. "Now we square off the edges, and then we cut the sheet into uniform strips about an inch wide. If you want to be precise, use one of the plastic rulers to mark your clay before you cut it, but you can usually just eyeball it and get a pretty nice set of strips." At least that's what the book had said. Maybe Bill was right. I probably should have made one of these myself ahead of time, but really, how hard could it be? I hoped this experiment didn't bite me, as some had in the past.

There was no turning back now. As confidently as I could, I said, "Lay half your strips out in one direction, keeping the edges pretty close together. Next, pick up another strip and start weaving it in and out of the strips you've laid out." I demonstrated briefly, and then I stopped working on mine so I could help them when they needed it.

"Now what?" Butch asked as he looked down at the woven mat. "It doesn't look like much, does it?"

"Now we bend it up on all four sides. Use

a rib to help the turn." A rib was a piece of wood or rubber — many times shaped like a large kidney bean — that helped the potter work clay. They came in various shapes and sizes, but I'd put out simple ones for our evening's work.

"I can't get it right," Sandy said as she stared at her lumpy basket.

"Let me see what I can do," I said. I worked the rib harder into the weave and managed to get a decent turn. "How's that?"

"Better, but the top's kind of ugly, isn't it?"

That's when I remembered I was supposed to have told them to save four strips to go along the perimeter to create a nice, finished edge. I started dismantling my bowl to supply them with the extra clay. "Use these to dress up the edges," I said as I handed out all but two of my own strips.

"But you don't get a basket this way," Jenna protested.

"I can make one whenever I want. So, what do you all think?"

They all agreed their baskets were nice, but they also wanted to try again.

"That's fine," I said, "but before we do, why don't we clean up so we can take your snack break?"

Butch nodded. "That's a great idea."

As we sat around the break table enjoying the meatballs and coffee from my new pot, Jenna asked, "Where's young David tonight? Does he have a class?"

"Yes, but I doubt he made it. He's still probably starry eyed about meeting Charles Potter."

"From what I've seen, he's good," Sandy said. "We ordered his book for the library, and I read it before we put it into circulation."

"Shame on you," Jenna scolded her lightly, obviously teasing her friend. "You should let your patrons have priority on the new books you get in."

"How can I honestly recommend a book if I haven't read it myself first?" Sandy asked, laughing. "Or movies, either, for that matter."

"I suppose you have a point," Jenna conceded. She turned to me and asked, "Have you read it, Carolyn?"

"I glanced through it earlier," I admitted as I pointed toward David's copy. "If you want my opinion, it's long on photographs and pretty short on technique. Just don't tell David I said that."

"There's no way that's his real name," Butch said as he glanced at the book.

"Why do you say that?" Jenna asked.

"Come on, a potter named Potter? Isn't that a stretch?"

"Not necessarily. I know a banker named Cash," Sandy said.

"And I know a farmer named Fields," I admitted.

"This sounds like a delightful game. What else can we come up with? A plumber named Flush?" Sandy asked.

"How about a carpenter named Woods?" Jenna asked, getting into the spirit of it. "It's your turn, Butch."

He frowned. "I just meant it sounded like an alias. I didn't mean to start something."

"Come on, don't be a spoilsport," Jenna said.

"Okay, give me a second," Butch said. "How about a construction crew chief named Foreman?"

"That's wonderful," Jenna praised him, and Butch decidedly glowed.

"How about a short-order cook named Frye?" I suggested.

"Or a golf pro named Link?" Sandy asked.

We were still coming up with names that matched their occupations when we heard the front door of the shop burst open. Goodness, had I forgotten to lock it after I'd let Jenna and Butch in?

It took only a second to realize that it was

someone who had a key. David rushed back to us, but before any of us could say a word, he said, "It's Charles Potter."

"What about him?" I asked as David fought to catch his breath.

"He's missing. He never showed up at the lecture, but they found his car. The door on the driver's side was standing wide open, and the keys were still in it."

"Where did they find it?" Butch asked.

David looked at me for a long few seconds, then said, "It was parked right in front of your house, Carolyn."

CHAPTER 2

"What on earth was he doing there? How did he even know where I live?" Honestly, I never went looking for trouble, but somehow it always managed to find me.

"You talked to him last night on the phone," David said. "Maybe it had something to do with that."

"I didn't give the man my home address. I don't even think I gave him my telephone number."

"Then why would he go there before he disappeared?" David asked, still looking at me askance.

"Are you under the impression that I had something to do with this?" I asked with more than a little edge in my voice.

"Take it easy, Carolyn, David's not accusing you of anything," Jenna said.

"Well, it surely sounded like it to me."

Sandy added, "He's just concerned. Carolyn, should you call Bill? Just to make sure he's all right?"

That hadn't even occurred to me. I dialed our home number, my fingers shaking as I punched the buttons. After seven rings, the machine kicked on. "Bill, it's me. Pick up. Bill. Bill? Call me as soon as you get this."

I hung up. "He's not answering. I'm going home."

"I'll go with you," Butch said.

"We'll all go," Jenna added.

The last thing I needed was a parade, especially if my dear husband was in the tub instead of lying dead or wounded on the kitchen floor. "I can manage."

Butch said, "Not without me."

"I'm coming, too," David said.

Sandy touched Jenna's arm. "Why don't we stay here and clean up? Would you like us to do that, Carolyn?"

"That would be great," I said as I grabbed my coat and my purse. If I were being honest with myself, I would have to admit I wasn't all that eager to go home alone.

Butch said, "Come on, we'll take my car."

I got into his Cadillac without a word of protest, and David climbed into the back seat. It wasn't much of a trip from Fire at Will to my house, but it seemed to take us a lifetime to get there. Parked in front of the house was Sheriff Hodges's patrol car, its lights flashing. The second we got there, I could see why Bill hadn't answered the telephone. He was standing right outside beside the sheriff, deep in conversation, and obviously surprised to see me tear up the road in someone else's car.

As I got out, Bill rushed over to me. "Are you all right? Is something wrong?"

"I was just going to ask you the same thing. When you didn't answer the phone, I got worried."

"So you brought the cavalry? Hey, Butch. How are you doing, David?"

David nodded an abrupt greeting as he approached Hodges. "Is there any sign of him? What happened?"

The sheriff ignored the question and stared at me. "What do you know about this, Carolyn?"

"I just heard about it," I said. "Is there any sign of him yet?"

Hodges shook his head. "One of your neighbors was out walking his dog when he found this car sitting here with the door open and the keys still in it. I was kind of hoping you might be able to shed a little light on it."

"I was at Fire at Will all evening," I said stuffily. "That car was certainly not there when I left." It was a beat-up Ford Escort, and I wondered how little the potter must have made publishing his opus.

"We can vouch for that," Butch said. "Not the car being there, but her presence at the shop. She never left the place all night, and I'm willing to swear to that in court."

"Why am I not surprised you'd vouch for her?" he said.

Bill piped up. "Wait a second here. We've already had this conversation, Hodges."

"It's *Sheriff* Hodges," the man said curtly.

"I've known you forty-five years, and I'll call you whatever I want. Carolyn didn't have anything to do with this."

The sheriff shook his head slightly. "I can't exactly just take your word for that, either, now can I?"

Bill looked like he was about to blow, and I didn't want the sheriff to have any more reason to dislike me or my family. "Why don't we go inside and let the police deal with it, Bill? I assume you're finished with us, Sheriff." The Firing Squad was just going to have to get along without me for the rest of the night.

"I'm done with you for now," he said. "I'll probably have more questions for you later. Right now, I've got my deputies coming. We're going to search the area for Mr. Potter."

"I'll help," David chimed in.

"Thanks, but we've got it covered," the sheriff said just as another squad car pulled up. He walked over to greet them.

I touched Butch's arm. "Thanks for bringing me home. Would you mind taking David back to the shop? I'd better hang around here for now."

"How are you going to get your car?" Butch asked.

"I'll take her later," Bill said. "Thanks for coming, both of you."

Butch nodded. "Call me if you need me. Don't worry about the time."

I smiled. "What about your appointment? I'd hate to interrupt anything."

"Friends come first," he said. Then Butch turned to David. "Let's go."

"I want to help look for him," my assistant said.

Butch replied, "I know you do, but the sheriff's already turned you down. Come on, there are bound to still be a few meatballs left back at Fire at Will."

Bill blanched a little at that, probably rightly believing he wouldn't be getting any leftovers tonight.

Once they were gone, my husband and I walked up to the house. "It's getting chilly, isn't it?" I asked. I glanced back at the abandoned car and added, "I hope he's all right."

"I just wonder what he was doing here in the first place," Bill said.

"I'm sure the sheriff is wondering the same thing," I said.

Once we were inside, Bill looked hard at me. "Are you sure you don't know why he'd come here?"

"I don't have a clue," I said. "And I'm not all that crazy about everybody asking me that. Why won't anybody believe me?"

"I do," he said gruffly. "I was just asking. It's too bad about the meatballs. I'm feeling a little peckish."

"You didn't look in the refrigerator, did you?" I walked into the kitchen and grabbed a covered dish. "I left you some, you big goof. All you had to do was look."

"Well don't just stand there, let's eat."

As Bill waited for the microwave to do its job on reheating our late snack, I asked, "Aren't you the least bit concerned about what happened to Charles Potter?"

"Why should I be? He's a grown man, isn't he? I'm sure he's fine."

"Then why would he just abandon his car like that, and what was he doing at our house in the first place?"

"I don't have a clue," Bill admitted as he

took the dish out of the microwave. He stabbed a meatball, ate it with relish, then asked, "Do you want one?"

"How can you eat at a time like this?"

"I can eat anytime," he said, "and if you want any of these, you'd better grab them now."

"I've lost my appetite," I said as I stared out the back window. I could see bobbing lights in the yard, and from the look of things, the sheriff had every deputy in the county searching for the lost potter. I just hoped when he did turn up, he'd be able to tell us what had happened, and why.

An hour later there was a tap on the door, and I jumped up to answer it. Sheriff Hodges looked upset, and I wondered what he'd found.

"Is he dead?" I blurted out. Probably not the best thing to ask the sheriff, but it had been weighing heavily on my mind.

"I have no idea. We couldn't find him."

Bill was right behind me. "If you want to search the house, you're going to have to get a warrant."

Hodges asked, "You'd actually make me do this the hard way? What are you hiding, Bill?"

I wanted to intercede, but I knew from

the set of my husband's jaw that the best thing I could do was get out of the way.

He wasn't even trying to keep his voice reasonable now. "I'm not hiding; I'm standing on my constitutional rights, and I'm telling you to your face. I'm not about to let you or anybody else bully me into doing something I don't want to do."

"Fair enough. Then we'll have to do this my way. I'll be back in half an hour with a search warrant, and in the meantime, there will be a deputy sitting in your living room."

"He can wait outside," Bill said.

This had gone far enough. "You both need to grow up. Come in and get it over with," I said.

"No," Bill snapped. "He's not going to parade in here acting like he owns the world."

"Hang on a second, Sheriff," I said. "We'll be right back." I closed the door and looked at my husband. "What has gotten into you? It's a reasonable request."

"I didn't like bullies in school, and I don't like them any better now. Carolyn, I'm surprised at you. I thought you despised that man."

"I'm the first to admit that I'm not his biggest fan, but he's got a job to do, and for once, it looks like he's actually trying to do it. If we get stubborn about this, we're costing the police time to make a more thorough search of the area. What if Potter is hurt, and he dies because nobody found him sooner just because we were posturing? How are you going to be able to sleep at night then?"

Bill returned my stare, then lowered his gaze. "Let him in, then."

"Not unless you agree to it, too. It's just as much your house as it is mine." I rubbed his shoulder gently. "I promise, you can chuck him out as soon as he looks through the place."

He grinned slightly. "I guess that's something."

He opened the door. "Come on in." As a deputy started to follow, Bill added, "Just you, Hodges."

The sheriff must have decided not to chide Bill about his means of address, or his demand. He turned to his deputy. "Wait here. I'll be right back."

"I should go in with you, sir."

The sheriff snapped, "What you should do is obey orders. In case you didn't hear me the first time, I said to wait outside until I'm finished."

Properly cowed, the deputy took a few steps back and Hodges came inside. After a quick but pretty thorough search of the place, he nodded once we got back to the front door. "Thanks for letting me cross this place off my list."

"Just let us know when you find out what happened to him," Bill said, the snap gone from his voice.

"Will do," Sheriff Hodges said as he left.

Once the door was closed again, I turned to my husband. "What happened? I thought you were going to rub his nose in the fact that Mr. Potter wasn't here."

"You were right. It would have been petty, and I'm a bigger man than that. What? I am."

"I never said a word," I said, trying to suppress my grin.

"Woman, are you looking to pick a fight with me?"

"Me? Not on your life. What are you going to do now?"

"What else is there to do?" Bill asked. "I'm going to bed."

"How are you going to sleep until they find out what happened to Charles Potter?"

He smiled at me. "Like a newborn with no conscience, a clean diaper, and full belly," he smiled.

I waited up, hoping for a knock on the front door during the night, but none came.

When I woke up the next morning on the couch, my neck was stiff, but sometime in the middle of the night my dear husband had covered me with a blanket. Why hadn't the old fool woken me up so I could sleep in my bed instead of out in the living room? I decided to give him credit for thinking of me at all. When I peeked out through the drapes in the front window, I saw that the police were gone, along with Charles Potter's car. What had happened to the man? I wanted to call Sheriff Hodges to see if he'd learned anything after he left us, but for once, my curiosity was defeated by my desire to keep the lowest profile I could. I'd been under the sheriff's suspicious gaze before, and I hadn't enjoyed it, not for one second.

"I don't think David slept more than an hour or two last night," Hannah said as we ordered coffees at In the Grounds before I opened Fire at Will. It was our ritual to meet at the coffee shop to start the day.

"I slept on the couch myself," I said as I rubbed my neck. "You're looking chipper, though."

Hannah was a slim brunette whose fortieth birthday was fast approaching, and I'd have to decide soon whether I was going to have a surprise party for her. When I'd turned forty, I'd invited the world to celebrate with me, whereas my husband had crawled into a hole the day before and had refused to come out for a week. I was still feeling Hannah out to see which reaction she was going to have, but so far, she'd neatly avoided all my queries.

"Am I?" she asked lightly.

"Hannah, what's up?" There was a gleam in her eye I hadn't noticed before.

"I'm sure I don't know what you're talking about," she said, but as she started to sip her coffee, I saw an unmistakable grin.

"Okay, give."

She shrugged. "If you must know, I have a date tonight."

I'd been badgering her for months to go out again. "How did that happen?"

"He asked, I agreed," she said smugly. "It's as simple as that."

"Do you really think I'm going to let you get away without more details than that?"

"Don't push me on it, Carolyn. I don't want to jinx it," she said.

"Fine, but I expect a full report when you get home, even if it's just long enough to change your clothes for work tomorrow."

"You've got a dirty mind," she said with a smile.

"One of us has to," I countered.

Hannah glanced at her watch. "I've got to run. I'll talk to you later."

"I'll be waiting by the phone."

As I walked to Fire at Will along the River Walk from the coffee bar, I marveled yet again at the foresight of our founding fathers. They had taken an average little stream called Pig Snout Creek, changed its name to Whispering Brook, then made the land beside it their retail shopping area, and all of this was done a great many years before San Antonio came up with their much showier River Walk.

"Hi, Rose. Is that new?" I called out to the proprietress of Rose Colored Glasses, a stained glass shop along the walk. Rose Nygren was a tall, skinny redhead with a complexion that would burn under a 40-watt lamp. She was standing in front of her shop, hanging a mobile made up of varied hues of colored glass.

"I'm wondering if it might attract more customers," she said, then turned to me and added, "Carolyn, the whole town's buzzing about what happened last night."

"Did I miss something?" I asked, knowing full well what Rose was referring to.

She raised one eyebrow. "From what I've

heard, you're right in the middle of it. Again."

"I can't help it if trouble seems to come looking for me." I studied her mobile, then added, "If you ever want to add any glazed pottery pieces to these, let me know. We could work something out, I'm sure."

She studied her creation a second, then said, "Let me think about it."

If Rose was aware of Charles Potter's disappearance the night before, then the rest of the town must know about it as well. That meant that Kendra Williams — the owner of Hattie's Attic and the biggest gossip in all of Maple Ridge, Vermont — was no doubt dying to grill me about what had happened. We'd been through an ordeal together earlier, and she'd been under the mistaken impression that we'd bonded. I didn't have the heart to tell her otherwise. Maybe if I hurried past her shop and kept my gaze on the creek, I could pretend not to see her, something hard to do, given her proclivity for wearing faded muumuus over her abundant frame, regardless of the weather or the temperature.

"Carolyn," she called out. "Carolyn!"

I'd have to have been deaf to not hear her. "Hi, Kendra. Sorry I can't stay and chat, but I've got to get to the shop."

41

"This will just take a second. Tell me all you know."

This woman was relentless. "That will take less time than what you've given me. I don't know anything about anything."

Would she buy it? I doubted it, even though it was the truth.

"Come on," she prodded in a stage whisper, "whatever you tell me will be just between the two of us."

For as long as it takes me to get inside my shop, I wanted to say, but didn't. Kendra had an information network that beat satellites and relay towers by a mile. I knew she would take the slightest gesture of mine and turn it into a full revelation without bothering with anything as mundane as the truth.

"Sorry, but it's the truth. I really don't know anything."

She was frowning at me as I brushed past her, but I was too deft to let her stop me. As I neared Fire at Will, I took in the tumbled brick exterior, the forest green awning with the shop's name written on it, the jet black front door, and the display window in front showing some of our best work to the world. In the window, I'd put out a lovely Japanese tea set my pottery instructor Robert Owens had made, a delicately painted porcelain Buddha Butch had decorated, an interesting vase Jenna Blake had created, and as always, a handful of my glazed and fired tree ornaments. It wasn't vanity that made me include my work with the others. I'd found early on that if I offered something inexpensive to average window-shoppers, I might be able to coax them to come in and browse our other offerings. If I was really lucky, they'd try their hand at painting some pottery of their own, the entire purpose of my business. I believed that painting pottery was not only fun but also therapeutic. The world was full of its own set of woes, and my shop offered a distraction from all of that.

"Have you heard anything?" David asked me before I even had the chance to walk into Fire at Will. "There's nothing on the news, and the paper just mentions finding his car."

"Did you go to the café and eavesdrop?" I asked as I stepped past my assistant into the shop. Shelly's Café was where many of the locals hung out, and I was certain if there was anything to learn outside of the sheriff's office, the café would be the place to hear it.

"I didn't think of that!" he admitted. "Do you mind if I go right now?"

"We open in fifteen minutes," I said,

glancing at the wall clock. It was a Salvador Dali–inspired piece that nearly dripped off its hook, something quirky that I was fond of, nevertheless.

The look of disappointment on David's face was too much to bear. "Be back in half an hour," I said.

"Thanks, Carolyn. You're the best."

"That's what I've been saying all along, but nobody seems to believe me," I said with a smile as he raced out the door.

I just hoped I'd have a quiet time of it until he returned. Of course, my hopes were dashed twelve minutes after he left.

The front door chimed, and I looked up to see a man in his early forties walking in the door. His face was vaguely familiar, and I tried to study him without being too obvious. He had a scruffy beard and long hair, and if it weren't for his nice clothes, I would swear he lived on the street.

"Aren't you even going to say hello?" he said.

The voice was even more familiar than the face. I looked past all the hair and realized who it was. "Richard Atkins. I thought you were dead."

Hannah's ex-husband and David's long-lost father was standing before me, and it was all I could do not to go for his throat. He'd deserted my best friend the second he'd found out she was pregnant, an act of cowardice that rated flogging in the town square, at least in my opinion. Then again, he was David's father, and if he'd come to see his son, to try to make some kind of amends for his desertion, I didn't want to be the reason he turned away.

Richard grinned. "A lot of folks probably have that at the top of their wish list, but so far, I've managed to disappoint them. How have you been?"

"Richard, do you honestly care?"

He shrugged. "Fair enough. Is David here?" He actually sounded nervous at the prospect of seeing his son.

"No, he's out at the moment. A potter disappeared last night, and he's trying to find him."

Richard ran his hands through his hair. "Sorry about that. I guess I kind of freaked out at the last second."

It took me a full ten heartbeats before I realized what he meant.

"Are you trying to tell me that you're Charles Potter?"

"One and the same," he admitted.

That was just a little too much, even for me. "Prove it."

He looked startled by the suggestion. "What do you want me to do, throw a pot? It's a pseudonym. My God, I thought everyone would see through it. I wasn't exactly trying to advertise my presence to the world, for a great many reasons."

Butch had seen through the obviousness of the name, at any rate. "Then why did you ever agree to come back here in the first place?"

"I was hoping to reconnect with my son," he said.

He had to be kidding. "In order to do that, you'd have to have some kind of connection with him to begin with, wouldn't you agree?"

"Hey, I was there at the very beginning."

"And then you left." Honestly, the man was insufferable. "Why on earth did you abandon your car in front of my house last night? The police thought I killed you and buried your body in my cellar."

"I thought you might be able to help me break the news to David and Hannah. But I couldn't ring the bell. I panicked, and I ran away. Sorry for the trouble."

I was about to snap at him when the door chimed.

It was David.

I hissed, "Don't say a word about who you

46

are, do you understand me?"

Richard looked puzzled. "Why not? That's why I came back in the first place."

"You wanted my help. Let me at least prepare him for this."

"Okay, if you think it's best."

David nodded to me, started to speak, then saw his father standing there. "Good morning," he said, then looked at me. "Nothing but idle rumor and speculation at the café."

"It was a long shot at best," I said, trying to find the words to introduce David to his father.

Richard saved me the trouble. "Hello, son."

David's face went white, and then without a word, he ran out of the shop.

CHAPTER 3

"I thought you were going to let me tell him," I said as I ran to the front door. Richard was right on my heels.

"I couldn't help myself. Where did he go?"

At first I couldn't see David, but then I caught a glimpse of his jacket as he ran down the River Walk. "We'll never catch him on foot."

"We can't just let him go."

"I don't know that we have much choice," I said. "Oh, no."

"What's wrong?"

I stared at him a second, then said, "I have to call Hannah. She needs to know what just happened."

"I'll call her if you want me to," he said.

"I think you've done enough damage for the moment," I said as I hurried back inside Fire at Will.

I tried Hannah's office, and I thought I'd missed her, but she picked up after the seventh ring.

"It's me," I said.

"Make it dance, Carolyn, I've got a class in seven minutes."

"Your ex-husband is back in town."

She must have dropped the phone, from the way it sounded. I asked, "Hannah? Are you all right?"

After a second, she came back on the line and said, "I'm fine. Where did you see him?"

"He's standing right in front of me. He came into my shop a few minutes ago, and before I could stop him, he introduced himself to David."

I heard nothing but silence on the other end of the phone, not even breathing. "Hannah, are you there?"

"What did David do?" she asked softly.

"He ran away. I'm sorry, I couldn't stop him. I thought you should know."

"Thanks. Let me talk to Richard."

I looked at him as I said, "Are you sure that's a good idea?"

"Put him on."

"Take it," I said to Richard, offering him the phone.

Richard looked as though he'd rather take a beating than my telephone, but after a few seconds, he accepted it.

I don't know what Hannah said to him,

but it must have been flame broiled. The man turned three shades of white, and then suddenly his face erupted in red before he handed the telephone back to me and started for the door.

"Where are you going?" I asked him as he rushed out.

"I'm going to find my son."

"Hannah, are you still there?" I asked into the receiver. Nothing. No doubt she'd hung up after delivering her scathing message.

I wanted to follow Richard and help find my assistant, but I had no idea where David might have gone, or what to say to him even if I did find him. There was nothing I could do but be there in case he came back to the shop.

I called Bill to tell him what had happened, but he didn't answer the phone. I left him a message to call me as soon as he got it, and hung up.

The door chimed just then, and I half-expected to see David or Richard walk in. To my surprise, it was Sheriff Hodges, and he had a scowl on his face that was darker than usual.

"I've got some news about that car," he said.

"It belongs to Richard Atkins," I said before he could continue.

"If you knew that, why didn't you tell me last night?" He looked angry enough to lock me up, which wasn't all that odd for him. "You could have saved me a great deal of time and energy."

"I just found out myself. He was here to talk to David."

"How did the boy react?"

"How do you think? He tore off like his shoes were on fire. He's never met the man."

The sheriff shrugged. "That's tough, but at least he's still alive."

"I'm not sure for how long. When I told Hannah her ex-husband was back in town, she was ready to kill him."

Hodges put his hand back on the front door. "Tell her to watch her temper. We don't need any more violence around here."

I rolled my eyes as he left, and wondered yet again how the man managed to get reelected time after time.

The phone rang, and it was Bill. "What's going on? I just got your message. Are you all right?"

"I'm fine. I thought you should know that I found out who really owned the car that was parked in front of our house last night."

"Did the sheriff come by and tell you?" he asked.

"I knew it before he did," I said, trying

not to sound too smug.

"Carolyn, have you been snooping again? That's a bad habit that's going to get you in big trouble someday if you're not careful."

"Thanks for the lecture. Now, do you want to hear what I found out or not?"

"I already know it belongs to Richard Atkins," he said.

"How on earth did you know that?" Honestly, the man drove me absolutely mad sometimes.

"The sheriff came by first and told me."

"Here's something I'm willing to bet you don't know," I said. "He's also Charles Potter."

"Who are you talking about? You don't mean Sheriff Hodges, do you? Have you been smelling fumes from the kilns again?"

"No, you nit, I'm talking about Richard Atkins. He made up the name to hide his identity."

Bill said, "Hannah's going to have little baby kittens when she finds out. Carolyn, I know how much you love to meddle, but stay out of this."

"It's too late for that. I already called her."

Bill sighed heavily. "How did she react?"

"She wants to kill him."

"You know what? I don't blame her a bit. Does David know?"

A customer walked in, and I held up a hand. "I'll be right with you," I said to her. "Bill, I've got to go."

"Did you tell David?" Bill asked again.

"No, Richard did that himself, right here in the shop. Good-bye, Bill."

"Call me right back," he said as I hung up.

"May I help you?" I asked my new customer.

The woman, a petite young thing who would probably be swallowed by a size 0, pointed to the display window. "I was wondering if you gift-wrapped."

"We can, for a nominal fee," I said. "Which piece are you interested in?"

She pointed to the Japanese tea set Robert Owens had created. "I'll take that."

"Wouldn't you like to know the price first?" Owens was charging an outlandish premium for the set, and I didn't want to shock the girl when I rang up the sale.

"It doesn't matter. It's for my mother. It's her birthday."

I told her the price just the same, but she didn't even flinch. "That's fine. When can I pick it up?"

Maybe I should have jacked the price up a little. I would make a nice commission on the sale, but every little bit helped. "I'll have it ready in ten minutes, if you can wait that long."

"I'd be delighted. I'll browse around while you wrap it."

I ran her card through the register, and after she signed the receipt, I boxed up the set and wrapped it. While I worked, she kept returning to the window for more items, and by the time I was finished ringing her up, she had just about wiped out the display. The only omission was my work. Out of everything she'd purchased, there wasn't a single ornament. In a fit of largesse, I retrieved one of my prettiest pieces and added it to her stack.

"I don't want that," she said.

"It's on the house," I said. "You get one free with every purchase over five hundred dollars."

She plucked it from the pile, a look of distaste on her face as she handed it back to me. "That's all right. If it's all the same to you, I'd rather not."

I wanted to kick her out onto the curb in that instant, but the commissions I'd make on the sales would more than make up for my hurt feelings. Plastering a smile on my face I didn't feel, I boxed everything up, and when she wasn't looking, I slipped the ornament back into one of her bags. What could she do, return it?

Hannah stormed into the shop two minutes after the young woman left. "Where's my son?"

"I wish I knew. Hannah, I'm so sorry. Richard just showed up and blurted out that he was David's father."

"I'll deal with him later," she said, with murder in her voice. "I just have to make sure David's all right first."

"He didn't come back here," I said. "You might want to call Annie."

I knew David's new girlfriend was a bone of contention between the two of them, but I never realized how deep the conflict was until Hannah said, "That's all right; I'll find him on my own."

"Swallow your pride and call her," I snapped. "She might be able to help, and you can't afford to be stubborn about this."

Hannah glared at me for several seconds, then calmly asked, "Do you have her number?"

"I can ask her if she's heard from David myself, if you'd like," I said as I dialed Annie's cell phone.

"No, that's all right. I'll talk to her," she said.

After a few moments of whispered conversation, Hannah handed the telephone back to me. "He's not with her, but she's going to call if he turns up."

As Hannah started to leave, I asked, "Where are you going?"

"I know his favorite places in Maple Ridge. If anyone can find him, I can."

I touched her arm lightly. "If you find Richard first, don't do anything rash."

"I'm not making any promises," she said, and then she was gone.

I hadn't even had the chance to tell her that Richard was going by the name Charles Potter, if it was indeed the truth. All of that would come out soon enough. Hannah was right. The only thing that mattered at the moment was that she find her son.

An older man with a luxuriant gray mustache and an elegant three-piece suit walked into the shop. "Are you open for business?"

"Certainly," I said. "How may I help you?"

"Are you sure you're open?"

Was he deaf? "Yes. Why am I having trouble convincing you of it?"

"Your front window's empty," he said, gesturing to the uncluttered space up front. I hadn't had a chance to restock the display.

"I'm trying to decide what to feature next," I said.

"I'd put something there, if I were you. I nearly passed on by the place."

"But you didn't, did you? Are you looking for a gift?"

He looked around. "Is this a gift shop? I thought it was a pottery painting place."

"It is," I said, though I couldn't imagine this man painting a bowl or a mug.

"I don't want to do that," he said stuffily.

"You don't want to buy anything or paint anything. I'm curious. Why exactly did you come in?"

"Perhaps I've made a mistake."

I had another thought. "If you're looking for a rifle or an antique pistol, you have."

He looked quizzically at me. "Now why on earth would you assume that?"

"It's the name," I said, gesturing to the sign out front. "Some folks think Fire at Will means we're a gun shop."

"Then they're idiots," he said soundly.

I still had no idea why he was in my shop, and I wondered if I'd ever know. I decided to wait him out, and thirty seconds later, he said, "I'd like to make something out of clay. You do that here as well, don't you?"

"Absolutely. We have pottery wheels in back."

"I have no desire to learn to throw pots," he said in his stuffy tone.

"Of course you don't."

He nodded. "I'm glad we understand each other."

I couldn't help myself. I laughed. "I haven't a clue what you're talking about."

"I want to build something from clay; a house, to be precise. Is that something I can do here?"

"I don't follow you."

He looked at me as if I were insane, grabbed a paper bag with "Fire at Will" emblazoned on it, then removed a pen from his suit pocket and proceeded to sketch out a house. "Here, this is what I want to do."

"What scale would you like to build this?"

"Life-size, of course," he said.

"It's a little more than I can handle in my kilns."

The man shook his head in obvious disgust. "Why does no one get my humor? I want to make something about the size of a tissue box."

"That we can do." I handed him an apron. "You need to put that on. I'd hate to get any clay on your suit."

He shunned the apron. "I'm most careful, I assure you. I won't need that."

"Suit yourself," I said. "I can help you with the basic shape, and then you can embellish it however you'd like. Fair enough?"

"I believe so."

I handed him a thick round dowel and a lump of clay. "You have to work the air out of that and get it ready."

He studied the clay in obvious distaste without touching it. "Would you mind?"

"Not at all." I kneaded the clay until it was a smooth consistency and handed it to him. The only problem was, he refused to take it. "What's next?"

"You have to roll it out," I said.

"Show me, please."

If he hadn't added the "please," I would have refused, but what else did I have to do at the moment? I rolled the clay out into a wide sheet until it was about a quarter of an inch thick, my favorite thickness for hand-building. "Now cut your walls and I'll show you how to put it together."

"I'm afraid I wouldn't be very good at that," he said.

Why wasn't I surprised? I cut the walls, floor, and roof out of three-quarters of the clay and quickly assembled the house. "I don't have any idea how you want to embellish this, but there are plenty of tools to cut out the shapes you'd like."

Instead of taking my not so subtle hint, he said, "Let me sketch out what I'd like."

He quickly embellished the house he'd

drawn earlier, adding window boxes, a grand front door, and a chimney along one side. "You can do this, can't you? Or is it too difficult?"

"I can do it all right. But I thought you came in here to do it yourself."

He said nothing, just kept staring at his drawing. I decided it would be easier to do it for him than argue with him about it, and after a few seconds, I nearly forgot he was there. I added the chimney and door, then started to cut out the windows.

"What are you doing?" he asked.

"I'm trying to match your windows."

"I want it to be solid," he said. "Can't you apply windows to the walls?"

"Sure," I said. He was awfully picky. "How's that?"

"Perfect," he said as he looked at the house. "Shouldn't there be shingles or something on the roof?"

"How about a thatched roof instead?" I was really getting into the model building.

"No, I'd prefer shingles."

I took my knife and scored in lines of shingles on the rooftop. "Is there anything else you'd like?"

He studied it a moment, then said, "No, it's perfect. Do we paint it now?"

"It has to be fired first. If you come back

in a few days, we can add the coloring then."

He frowned. "Does it really take that long?"

"I have to wait until I have a full kiln," I explained. "It's too expensive to fire a single item."

"I see," he said as he dipped his hand into his jacket. And why shouldn't he? The man hadn't bothered to dirty his hands the entire time he'd been in my shop. He retrieved an eel-skinned wallet and plucked a brand new hundred from it. "Will this cover your firing fee?"

"I think so," I said as I accepted the bill.

"Good. Then I'll see you this time tomorrow."

He was gone before I could even get his name, but if he wanted to be anonymous, he was paying for the privilege. I had a few other pieces to fire, so I decided to do a bisque-firing immediately. It was against my normal policy, but then again, I wasn't in the habit of hand-building projects for my customers, either. If it paid that well all the time, I'd have to start, though. I was just about to close the kiln and turn it on when I realized that I really wanted to see what the cottage would look like with a thatched roof. No one was in my shop, so I had time to make a cottage of my own. I set to work, creating a cottage completely different from that my customer had designed, and the results pleased me. Maybe I'd have to add a building segment to one of my classes.

My stomach growled as I turned the kiln on, and I realized that I'd nearly missed lunch. With no prospect of David's return, I had two choices: I could either raid the paltry contents of my shop pantry, or I could shut the place down and go get a decent lunch. If I hadn't just earned that hundred-dollar firing fee, I might have made do with the remnants in my shop, but that bill was pure profit as far as I was concerned, and I was determined to spend it. Normally every dime I made went into my shop books, but this once, I was going to make an exception. There was a hat I'd been admiring on my strolls past Hattie's Attic, and though I wasn't all that eager to do business with that busybody Kendra Williams, I did think it would look smart on me. I got out the sign that said, "Gone to Lunch," put it in the store window, and locked up.

As I glanced back inside to see if I'd left any lights on, I noticed just how stark the front window really was. My gentleman customer had been right. It wasn't very inviting; it made the shop look more like a place for lease than a going concern. My stomach growled again, but I ignored it and headed back inside.

Grabbing what I could from the sales area, I filled up the window without too much concern for themes or even basic principles of display. The window was full again, that was what really mattered, and I could go eat with a somewhat clear conscience.

I'd planned on trying the hat on after I ate, but if I was going to avoid Kendra until then, I was going to have to stear clear of Hattie's Attic. It was amazing how often I ate lunch at Shelly's Café simply because it was located in the opposite direction from Kendra's shop.

"Carolyn Emerson, have you been avoiding me?" Though she was busy grilling for her big lunch crowd, Shelly Ensign took the time to wave a spatula at me as I walked into the café. She was a petite woman, but anyone who had ever been on the other side of one of her tongue lashings knew her small size belied her feisty personality. I'd gone to school with Shelly, and not only had we sat beside each other in alphabetically ordered classrooms, but we also had consecutive birthdays: Shelly's birthday was May 11, mine, May 12.

"Shelly, why on earth would you ask me that?"

"You haven't been here in a week. Did I say something to offend you?"

"Nothing out of the ordinary," I replied as I took a seat at the counter that stood between the grill and the other tables. The café had last been decorated sometime in the 1950s, sporting black and white scuffed tiles, red vinyl tabletops, and mismatched chairs, the motif worked for Shelly.

Ken Marcus, the town's only doctor and the man who had delivered both of us, said, "Wait a second, you two are nearly exactly the same age. Yes, I remember that May well. Shelly, you were born at 11:57 p.m., and then I had to rush over to the next room to deliver you, Carolyn. It was 12:06 a.m., if I remember correctly."

"Nothing wrong with his mind," Shelly said.

"He's as sharp as ever," I added.

"Are you two youngsters making fun of me?" Dr. Marcus asked.

"Us? Why, we'd never do that," Shelly protested.

"No, sir, not for one second."

The good doctor stared hard at each of us in turn, threw a ten-dollar bill down beside his plate, and then headed for the door.

"One of you bit me right after you came out, but I won't say which one did it."

Shelly and I pointed at each other automatically and said in near-perfect unison, "It had to be her."

The doctor shook his head and walked out without another word.

I looked at Shelly, fighting to hold my laughter in, but the second her smile broke free, I couldn't restrain myself. I didn't care that some of the other customers in the café were looking at us a bit oddly. It felt good to laugh.

"What can I get you today?" she asked as she went back to her grill.

"I'll have my usual." I thought about facing a salad on what I'd dealt with so far that day, and changed my mind. "On second thought, give me a hamburger and some French fries."

"Do you want a chocolate shake to go with that?"

"No, I'd better not. Make it a Coke. Diet."

Shelly smiled. "Sure, because you wouldn't want any unnecessary calories, now would you?"

"What can I say? I'm watching my figure."

She let that slide, so I asked her, "Are you feeling okay?"

"Why, what have you heard?"

"You let an opening like that sneak past you, I'm ready to call the paramedics."

"We're right here if you need us," a handsome young man said from a table in the back. I hadn't spotted him coming in, but sure enough, he and his partner were wearing EMT uniforms.

"False alarm," I said.

He nodded, and they went back to their meals. I turned back to Shelly. "I mean it, what's gotten into you?"

"Wayne thinks I'm too much of a smart aleck."

Wayne Campbell was her latest boyfriend, a man eleven years her junior. I would never dream about teasing her about that, though. Shelly had lost her first husband to cancer and the second to a car accident. I figured my friend was entitled to whatever happiness she could find. "Tell Wayne I like our relationship just fine the way it is," I said with a smile.

She nodded. "I do, too. Let me get that food for you."

I looked around the café as I waited for my order. It was jammed full with folks from town. There were restaurants where the tourists liked to go, but Shelly's was for locals. Not to say we'd throw somebody out if they weren't from Maple Ridge, but it took a brave soul to look past the rundown exterior of the café and actually step inside. I saw the mayor having lunch with his secretary from the car dealership he owned, and I wondered who they thought they were fooling with their innocent act. They were involved in something — romantics would call it a love affair; more pragmatic types would label it a sleazy relationship on the side. Either way, I doubted they'd be able to get away with it much longer. As some folks around our parts liked to say, "There's a storm a brewing."

Shelly slid my burger and fries in front of me, well before I was due to get my food. I lowered my voice. "You didn't have to bump my place in line."

"You've got a business to run, and no one to help you at the moment. I don't hear any complaints, do you?" She gazed around her restaurant, and not another glance met her stare.

"You heard about David already?"

Shelly nodded. "The whole town knows about it by now. Imagine the nerve of Richard Atkins just showing up like that. He ought to be shot, and I've heard a few folks think he will be."

"David and Hannah would never do

anything like that, no matter what the provocation."

Shelly shrugged. "Who's to say what folks would do, given the right circumstances? Don't forget, though, Richard Atkins has more enemies in Maple Ridge than his exwife and his son."

"Like who, for instance?" I asked. I was not normally a gossip. Well, I wasn't. Okay, I admit that I might have shared a tidbit or two in the past, but this was different. Well, it was.

Shelly nearly whispered as she spoke next, and I had to strain to hear her. "There are a few folks sitting right here, our dear mayor being one of them."

I looked at Harvey Jenkins, who kept his rapt gaze on his curvy secretary, Nancy Jane Billings. "What could Harvey have against Richard?"

"You didn't know? They were in some kind of business together, and when Richard disappeared, evidently he took some of Harvey's money with him."

That was interesting, and something I'd never heard about. "Who else?"

Shelly looked toward the front door. I turned to see Kendra Williams making her way to the café. "Speak of the devil and she appears. Kendra has a reason of her own to make him regret showing up here."

"Kendra? Don't tell me she and Richard had anything in common."

Before Kendra could get inside, Shelly said softly, "Some folks say Richard did the antiquing on some of her pieces and started blackmailing her when she balked at paying him for his silence."

"That was a long time ago," I said.

"You know what they say. Elephants don't forget."

That was a cheap shot at Kendra's weight, but I wasn't about to defend her, not after Shelly had scalded me so many times with her whiplash tongue.

"Who else?" It was fascinating to me that I'd missed so much dirt.

"Can't talk about it now," Shelly said.

There was an empty stool beside mine, and I knew Kendra would head straight for it. Could I stop her somehow? Tell her it was saved for Bill, or someone else? Knowing Kendra, I was sure she'd stand there and wait, and when no one showed up, she'd start in on me. My best option would be to wolf down my food so I'd be exposed to her for a minimal amount of time.

"Is this taken?" she said loudly in my ear.

"Feel free," I said as I jammed a large bite

into my mouth. "I'm just about through here."

"Don't hurry on my account," she said.

Shelly asked, "What can I get you?"

"The usual," she said. I wondered what that might be, but not enough to hang around to see for myself.

Kendra somehow managed to settle her bulk onto the counter stool and said, "It's a terrible shame about poor David, isn't it?"

"What about him?" I said through the fistful of fries I had crammed into my mouth. These weren't the skinny little fast-food fare, either. They were honest potato wedges, and I could barely mumble with them in my mouth.

"Imagine, that father of his just showing up like that after twenty years. He took off about the time the jewelry store was robbed, didn't he?"

I somehow managed to swallow, and said, "I guess so. I understand you knew Richard pretty well back then."

Kendra's eyes narrowed. "Who told you that?"

"I can't remember," I lied, trying not to look at Shelly.

"It's a bold-faced lie," Kendra snapped. "And I don't want to talk about it."

That was a switch. I didn't think there was

anything on the planet Kendra wouldn't discuss. I thought about pressing her further, but if I did, it would have to wait. I ate the last bite of my burger, slipped my payment under my plate, then turned to Shelly and said, "Thanks for lunch."

She pointed to my money. "There'd better be enough for a tip in there, too."

"You know me, I always tip a solid 9 percent," I said with a grin.

Shelly collected the money as she cleared the plate. "It's nice to have something in this world I can count on."

I walked outside, grateful for the respite from the noise in the café. It hadn't sounded that loud when I was inside among them adding my own voice to the fray, but it became extremely noticeable once I was away from it. I didn't know how Shelly took it all day.

I thought about the hat I'd wanted to look at in Kendra's shop, but as she was at the café, I knew Hattie's Attic was closed. Now that my belly was full, I was starting to feel guilty about shutting my shop, especially with David missing. Had he come back while I'd been gone? I found myself hurrying back to Fire at Will. The sign was still in the door, and the place was dark inside. If he'd come back, he hadn't bothered opening up.

"David?" I called out as I walked inside after unlocking the door. I had the weirdest feeling, as if expecting to find a dead body in my shop. To be frank, it had happened before, though I hadn't had a premonition about it as I was now. A part of me wanted to call Bill, or even the sheriff, but I had no idea what I would say to either one of them. One thing I knew for sure. I wasn't about to admit that I had a gut feeling that something was wrong. I could hear them now, cackling about woman's intuition, something I believed in wholeheartedly, and I wasn't in the mood to be teased or scorned for it.

"David, are you back there?"

Still no reply. I wasn't convinced the place was corpse-free until I'd searched every bit of space big enough to hold a body.

Carolyn, I chided myself after shutting a closet door, you are letting your imagination take control of you.

I turned on the lights, flipped the sign to "Open," and tried to get rid of that sick, dull feeling that was still lingering in the pit of my stomach. I called David's cell phone, and then Hannah's, but I got their voice mails. Had my friend managed to find her son, or were they both ignoring any summons from the world outside their own? I hoped Hannah had found him, or would soon. She'd be able to settle David down. At least I hoped she could.

Blast Richard Atkins anyway. What nerve he had showing up like that after all those years. I was still cursing him under my breath when the telephone rang.

It turned out to be a call I wasn't particularly pleased to receive.

CHAPTER 4

"Sheriff, I don't know anything I haven't already told you," I said for the third time in the conversation. "David's still gone, and so is Richard. I haven't heard from Hannah, either. Why the sudden interest in their lives?"

"It's not all that sudden," he said. "I don't want this to develop into more than it has to. If you hear from any of them, call me."

"You'll be the first one on my list," I said, not even trying to sound sincere.

"That's good," he said, apparently missing my sarcasm. "I'd hate to see somebody get hurt."

"For once we have something we can agree on."

Without another word, he hung up. I had half a mind to call him back, but then the telephone rang.

"Where have you been?" My husband started in on me before I could get out an answer. "You were supposed to call me right back."

"I got distracted," I said. "It's been crazy here."

"Okay, I understand. Let me take you out to lunch, then. I'm starving."

"I really can't leave the shop right now," I said, failing to admit that I'd already eaten.

"Then I'll bring you something. How about a hamburger from Shelly's Café?"

There was no way I was going to put my friend in the position of lying to my husband for me. "I had one a few minutes ago," I admitted.

"I thought you were too busy to eat." His voice had that distinct sullen tone I knew all too well.

"I'm sorry, I should have called you back. I was wrong. Forgive me?"

Sometimes, the only thing to do is throw oneself on the mercy of the court.

To my delight, my husband accepted my apology. "If you had a burger, I'm getting one, too. And fries. And a shake."

"Hey, I had a Diet Coke with mine."

"Tough for you," he said with just a little too much glee in his voice.

"Enjoy your meal," I said. After all, being gracious in return was the least I could do.

"And pie," he added before he hung up. I

thought about calling Shelly and vetoing the dessert, but Bill had probably earned it.

I was trying to figure out a new way to arrange the front window when I looked up to see Hannah tearing down the street. I raced out onto the sidewalk, but she blew past me, nearly knocking me over.

"Hannah? What's wrong?" I yelled at her back.

"I can't talk right now, Carolyn," she said, barely turning around.

"What is it? Did you find David?"

She didn't answer. In all the years I'd known her, I'd never seen my best friend act like that. Did it mean that she'd finally caught up with David, or had she found Richard instead?

This insanity had gone on much too long for my taste. It was time to call out the reinforcements. That meant the Firing Squad, my team of amateur potters, as well as one of the best informal investigation crews in our part of Vermont. If they couldn't find David, I wasn't sure what I would do, but at least we had to try. Butch answered on the first ring.

"Are you waiting for a call?" I asked him after I identified myself.

"I had a feeling you'd be giving me a

ring," he said. "I haven't seen him."

"How on earth did you know I was looking for David?"

"Give me some credit, Carolyn," he said with a chuckle. "I know more about what goes on here than I let on. I've asked a few friends to keep an eye out for him, too, but so far, no luck."

"I appreciate your help," I said. "I need to call Jenna and Sandy, too."

"It's taken care of," Butch said. "I'm coordinating things from here, and I'll let you know as soon as any of us hear anything."

"I feel useless," I admitted. Butch had taken it upon himself to organize a search party, probably while I'd been stuffing my face at Shelly's.

"Don't say that," he said. "We need you."

"That's sweet of you to say, even if it's not true."

"Don't sell yourself short, Carolyn." He hesitated a second, then said, "We probably shouldn't tie up the line."

"I thought you'd have call-waiting," I said.

"I do, but the last time I checked, you didn't. What happens if David tries to call you and gets a busy signal?"

"I hadn't thought about that. I'd better get off." I hung up. I'd have to thank Butch for his efforts by making a batch of my peanut butter and Hershey's Kiss cookies. He'd loved them since the first time I'd brought a batch to one of our meetings, and every now and then I liked to surprise him with the treats. He'd earned a double batch today.

I waited on a few customers, but the day still dragged. I kept expecting David to walk in. I had a funny fluttering in my stomach, and it wasn't because of anything I'd eaten at Shelly's. I feared something had happened to my young assistant. The phone rang a dozen times during the rest of the afternoon. The Firing Squad kept checking in, all with null reports, unfortunately.

It was seven minutes past my regular closing time, but I couldn't bring myself to lock the door and go home. What if David needed me, and I wasn't there?

The door chimed, and I called out without looking up, "We're closed."

"You're not, but you should be," my husband, Bill, answered.

"What are you doing here? I thought you'd be ankle deep in sawdust." He was busy working on new furniture pieces for Shaker Styles, a local furniture business, and I'd grown accustomed to his late hours.

"I was. Now I'm not. Let's go home."

"Are you telling me you stopped work to take me home? I'm not some kind of feeble old invalid who needs watching after."

He frowned. "That's not what I meant. I've been working too hard lately. I miss you."

What a sweet old bear. I hugged him, then said, "That's one of the nicest things I've ever heard you say. What exactly do you miss most about me?"

"Well, the first thing that comes to mind is that I haven't had a home-cooked meal in weeks," he said.

I jerked away from him. "And you're not getting one tonight." He had a decidedly crooked smile when I looked at him. "Why are you grinning like an old fool?"

"I was just kidding."

"Well, it wasn't very funny."

He shrugged. "You were fishing for compliments. You know how I hate that. Come on, let's go home."

I could have fought him on it, but he was right. We hadn't been spending much time together lately, and I'd missed him, too. "I don't know if I should leave."

"I said I was sorry."

He looked hurt. "Actually, you didn't. But that's not why I want to stay. What if David needs me and I'm not here?"

"He knows where we live, Carolyn," Bill said. "If he finds this place empty, we're less than ten minutes away. Come on, I'll make you dinner tonight."

I wasn't in the mood for one of his evening breakfast meals. "Thanks for the offer, but I've had stew simmering away all day."

"That beats my eggs, I won't deny it. Let's go."

I looked around the shop, still not sure if I should leave. But Bill had a point. I had no idea if David would show up, and it didn't make sense for me to wait for him. "Let me just do a few things to close, and then I'll meet you at home."

"I can wait," he said.

"Are you going to just stand there and hover while I work?"

"No," he said. "I think I'll sit down instead."

My husband dead-bolted the front door, flipped the "Open" sign to "Closed," then walked to the back of the shop and flopped down on the new couch. It had been an extravagant splurge, but one I'd happily made, eager to replace its predecessor.

I took the day's receipts from the till, totaled the report, then slid everything into my store safe — a ceramic piggy bank. It wasn't all that secure if someone knew where to look, but honestly, who would look in a piggy bank in a pottery store for money?

"Let's go," I said as I finished my nightly tasks.

"Do you have a firing tonight?"

"No, I've got one going already, and I'm waiting until tomorrow for the other one."

"Good enough. Let's go get some stew."

Out on the sidewalk, I bolted the door and turned to my husband. "Whose car should we take?"

Bill smiled at me. "You'd better drive. I went home and parked my truck, then I walked back here."

"What's gotten into you?" I asked. My husband wasn't exactly an exercise fanatic. "It must have taken you an hour to get here on foot."

"More like half that," he said smugly. "It was a pretty evening, and I've been stuffed inside that woodworking shop too much lately. I needed some fresh air."

"You're perfectly welcome to walk back home, then."

He raised an eyebrow. "There's no need to be obsessive about it. Let's go."

The first thing I did when we walked in the door at home was check our answering machine. It was dismally blank. I'd hoped that David would have at least checked in, especially given his hasty exit from the shop, but I knew he wasn't obligated to call. Even our sons didn't call us regularly. Bill and I had raised our boys to be independent, to live their lives on their own. Some of my friends demanded daily or weekly calls and visits from their children, but I thought they were a bit daft. I, for one, refused to wait by the phone. I had a life of my own to live, and while I loved my two boys more than anything in the world, besides my husband, I was proud of them for making their own way in the world. Birthdays, holidays, and a few times in between were usually the only occasions when we heard from them.

"Nobody writes, nobody calls," Bill said as he caught me staring at the phone.

"No news is good news," I said. The aroma coming from the kitchen was divine. "Let's eat, shall we?"

"I'm one step ahead of you. I already set the table."

After we ate, Bill asked, "How about a movie?"

"You're actually staying here? What about those deadlines?"

"They can wait. I want to spend a little time with you, and to be honest, I'm flat worn out. So, what would you like to watch?"

"We haven't seen *Casablanca* in a while," I suggested.

"Bogart it is," he said.

The movie hadn't even flashed back to Paris before Bill was sound asleep. Truthfully, it wasn't holding my attention, either, and I thought it was the greatest movie of all time. I nearly turned it off, but then remembered Bill's reaction to silence. As long as the movie played on, he wouldn't stir, but if I turned it off, or even lowered the volume, he'd shoot out of his chair as though it were on fire. I grabbed a light sweater, tucked the portable phone in my hand, then went outside. The Vermont summer was fast approaching, by far my busiest season of the year. Not only did tourists descend on Maple Ridge, but also the town's children were out of school, so I would have summer camps and classes going almost continuously. We needed the cash influx to stay open the year round, but I didn't look forward to the rapid pace life would soon hold.

I hadn't done a raku firing in some time, and I realized I'd like to. The electric kilns did a fine job back at the shop, but the raku process was simple and offered spectacular results. I'd take pieces we'd already bisque fired, then after glazing them, bring them to my backyard, where I had my equipment set up. After a quick firing in my outdoor gas-fed brick kiln, I'd pull out the red-hot pots and bury them in wood shavings or wadded-up newspaper. Thermal shock caused the glazes to shrink and crackle. It was a process I loved, partly because there was no way to exactly predict what the outcome would be. Oh, I'd have an idea of what the end result would look like, but it almost never completely matched the finished product.

Leaves had collected in the pit area where I moved the pieces after their firings; I'd need to clean up the area if I was going to fire again.

As I walked closer to the pit, I noticed the leaf pile had a peculiar shape to it. It was as if — no, it couldn't be. I brushed a few leaves from the pile, and my worst fears were confirmed.

It was a body, and the instant I saw the man's long hair, I knew it was David.

"Bill, wake up. Call the sheriff."

"What?" he asked groggily as he sat up. "What happened?"

"Where's the phone?" Why wasn't he

84

listening to me?

"Take it easy, Carolyn. It's right there in your sweater pocket."

I'd forgotten I had it. My fingers were shaking too much to dial the numbers, and I shoved it into his hand. "Call Hodges. I found David. By the kiln. He's dead." The sobs were coming now, stealing my breath, and to my husband's eternal credit, he ignored the phone and wrapped me up in his arms. After a few minutes, I managed to catch my breath and I pulled away from him. "Sorry. I lost it for a second there."

"You're entitled. Are you going to be all right?"

"I think so," I muttered.

"Good. Stay right here. I'll be back in a second."

The last thing in the world I wanted was to be left alone. "Where are you going?"

"I have to check myself."

"You don't believe me?" My voice had a hysterical pitch, but I couldn't seem to suppress it.

"Of course I do. It won't take a second."

"I'm going with you," I said.

"You don't need to."

"You're wrong. I do."

He studied me a second, then said, "Come on."

Why on earth had I volunteered to see David again? I couldn't decide which was worse, the prospect of seeing Bill turn him over and staring into David's lifeless eyes, or being in that house alone, waiting for my husband to return.

"Let me grab my flashlight," he said. A minute later, we were outside by my kiln. I wondered if I'd ever be able to bring myself to fire there again. I doubted it, with the image of David constantly hovering in my mind.

I stayed back a few paces, but Bill walked up to the body and knelt beside it. "What are you doing?" Why was I screaming?

"I've got to make sure he's really dead."

Oh no. I hadn't even considered that possibility. What if my reaction had robbed David of his last chance to be saved? Hannah would hate me for eternity, and I wouldn't blame her.

My husband reached down and tried to find a pulse. I stood there watching, afraid to utter a word.

He shook his head, then stood. "He's dead all right, but it's not David."

"Are you sure? The hair looks just like his."

Bill said, "That's because you looked at it in the twilight. It's too gray to be David's, but unless I'm missing my guess, it's his father."

I felt a momentary flood of relief wash through me, but it was soon gone.

"What's wrong?" Bill asked me. "I thought you'd be happier about the news."

"I'm glad it's not David, but you know who the sheriff is going to suspect. Hannah had every reason in the world to kill him, didn't she?"

"From what I've heard around town, she'd have to get in line." He started dialing the phone, but I put a hand on his. "Do we have to call him right now?"

"You know we do," Bill said. "It's the proper thing to do."

"I guess," I said, "but I'd like to see if I can get Hannah first and warn her about what's about to break loose."

"It'll have to wait until I call Hodges," my husband said firmly.

Thirty seconds later, after listening to Hodges's warning not to touch anything, Bill handed me the phone. "I'd call her as fast as you can. You're right; she deserves a heads up about what's about to happen."

At least my hand wasn't shaking anymore. I dialed Hannah's number, and instead of saying hello, she answered with a question. "David, is that you?"

"It's Carolyn," I said. "I'm afraid I've got some bad news for you."

"It's David, isn't it? He's dead." There was an utter lack of emotion in her voice as she said it, as if she already believed it in her heart.

"I found a body, but it wasn't your son's. It's Richard. Somebody killed him and his body is in my backyard."

"Oh, no," she said, and then hung up the telephone before I could warn her that the sheriff would likely be coming after her and her son.

Bill asked, "What did she say?"

"As soon as I told her about Richard, she hung up on me."

He shook his head. "I hope she doesn't run away from this. Panicking is the worst thing she could do right now."

"She didn't kill her ex-husband," I snapped at Bill.

"Take it easy. I didn't say she did. But you know how she can be."

I was saved from answering by the sound of sirens nearing. A minute later, Sheriff Hodges came into the backyard, followed by half a dozen other officers.

"You can go inside," he said to us after he heard how I'd stumbled across the body. "I'll be in later to get an official statement from you."

"I just told you all I know," I said.

"Bill, will you take her inside? We've got work to do."

He nodded and put an arm around me. "Come on, Carolyn. Neither one of us can do anything out here."

"You're taking orders from the sheriff now?"

He whispered, "I'm doing this for you. Do you really want to see them examining the body? I thought I'd save both of us from that nightmare."

"Okay, I understand that."

I walked inside with my husband, who said, "You might want to put a pot of coffee on. It's getting chilly out there."

"They can go to the convenience store and get their own coffee," I said.

"They can, or we can do the right thing and offer them something ourselves. Carolyn, I know you don't like the man, but it wouldn't hurt to be civil. He's just doing his job."

"I'm not sure I agree with that."

"Blast it all, I'll make it myself then." As Bill started toward the coffeepot, I waved him off. "I'll do it. After all, I don't want them to arrest you."

"Why would they do that?"

"Some folks might think having to drink your coffee was a crime."

At least it gave me something to do. After the coffee had brewed, Bill grabbed a tray and filled it with mugs, and I got the pot.

To my relief, the body was gone by the time we got out there. The sheriff said, "I thought I told you to stay inside."

"We brought you and your staff some fresh coffee," I said as I took in the scene: crime tape surrounded my kiln, portable lamps lit up the yard, and an officer was filming the whole thing.

"That would be nice," he admitted as he took a mug from me.

"So, do you know what killed him yet?" I asked as casually as I could manage while Bill handed out mugs to the rest of the force.

"Is that why you're suddenly being so nice?" he asked. "Are you out here trying to mine me for information?"

"Forget I said anything," I said.

After a few sips of coffee, Sheriff Hodges said, "Sorry. Murder always puts me on edge. I'd tell you if I could, but it's not time to release that information yet." He gestured with the cup. "Thanks for the brew."

"You're welcome," I said.

After he was finished, he handed me the mug. "That was mighty hospitable of you,

Carolyn."

"It was Bill's idea," I admitted.

"Tell him I said thanks, then." He paused and said, "He was beaten up pretty bad." Then asked, "Did David ever turn up?"

"You honestly can't suspect him of killing his own father, can you?"

He paused a second before answering. "There's no telling what a shock like that might do to his system. Now, don't get in an uproar. I need to talk to him, that's all. Surely you can see that yourself. How about Hannah? Why isn't she here?"

"What do you mean?"

"Carolyn Emerson, I'll give you ten to one that you called her right after your husband called me. Don't make me pull the phone records to prove it."

"What makes you think I didn't call her before I called you?"

"I doubt Bill would let you. So let me ask you this. Why isn't she here? She's got a stake in it — even you have to admit that."

"I don't know what you're talking about," I said as I turned and walked away.

As Bill and I collected the rest of the mugs, I did my best to avert my gaze from the raku pit. It was as dead to me now as Richard Atkins.

My thoughts returned to David. His

disappearance would look bad for him, but why would David kill Richard? The man was his father, albeit an absentee one. Then I realized that Richard, in the guise of Charles Potter, had also been his hero. There was no telling what he might do given that combination. Could Hannah have killed him? She had reason enough. At least she had twenty years ago. But that was a long time to hold a grudge. Or was it? There had to be other suspects, including the ones Shelly had mentioned earlier that day. I wondered if the mayor, Harvey Jenkins, or that gossip Kendra Williams had alibis for this evening, or if Sheriff Hodges would even get around to asking them. No, most likely he'd focus on David and Hannah, two of my favorite people in the world. I was not going to let him pin this murder on either one of them. Whether Bill liked it or not, that meant that I was going to have to do a little digging on my own.

CHAPTER 5

"I'll see you this evening," I told my husband the next morning after I kissed his cheek.

"Where are you going at this hour?" he asked as he sat up in bed. "It's the middle of the night."

"It's 6 a.m.," I corrected him. "I have some errands to run before I open Fire at Will."

"Hang on a second. Let me get dressed and I'll go with you." He started to get up, and I put a hand on his shoulder.

"Go back to sleep. I'm perfectly capable of being on my own."

He rubbed his eyes. "Have you talked to Hannah already?"

"No, but I'm hoping she meets me for coffee this morning. She usually calls to cancel if she can't make it, and I never heard from her last night." I was painfully aware of the extenuating circumstances that might have kept her from calling, but that didn't mean I was going to give up on my friend. I was hoping the regularity of our morning coffee breaks together would bring her to In the Grounds out of habit, if nothing else.

"Who are you going to talk to this early?"

"No time to chat. I'll call you later." I knew if I told my husband I was going to Shelly's Café, he'd refuse to stay home in bed. He loved her pancakes more than he loved mine, a point of contention between my dear husband and me since he'd first disclosed it.

Shelly looked surprised to see me as she worked at feeding what was currently a light breakfast crowd. "I didn't know your alarm clock worked," she said as she slid three eggs, bacon, and a short stack of pancakes on a platter.

"I'll have one of those," I said.

"I don't care what you get, but you can't have that one," a burly man said from the other end of the counter. "That one's mine."

"Or is it?" Shelly asked. "How do you know Carolyn didn't phone ahead?"

"You don't take telephone orders," he said smugly.

"I do for my friends," she replied.

He looked as though he might cry.

"Let him have it," I said. "I'll wait my turn."

For a moment, I thought the man was actually going to kiss me. "Thanks."

"My pleasure," I said.

Shelly leaned forward. "Is that really what you want?"

"Make it two eggs, one piece of bacon, and some dry toast," I said, vowing to stick to my diet.

"Not even one pancake?" she asked.

"Well, just one," I said, promising myself I'd try walking home sometime myself.

She had my breakfast ready in no time, and since no other customers had come in, Shelly pulled up a stool and sat across from me at the counter. "Mind some company?"

"Actually, I was hoping to talk to you."

She nodded. "The sheriff came by. I figured the murder last night brought you in this morning. It must have been awful finding the body like that."

"It wasn't the most pleasant thing I've ever experienced," I admitted, "but at least it wasn't David." I explained the similarities between David's and his father's hair colors and styles, and my confusion when I'd stumbled into the pit the night before.

"I never even thought of that," she said. "Have you seen him? How's he taking it?

It's got to be tough losing a father you didn't even know."

"I haven't talked to him, or his mother. It wouldn't surprise me if the sheriff has them both locked up by now."

Shelly frowned. "I know you're not a big fan of the man, but he's not as bad as you think."

"I don't know how he could be," I said. "The real reason I'm here is that I'm looking for more information."

"About Richard Atkins? Carolyn, I don't know anything I could swear to. All I hear are rumors and idle speculation around this place. You'd be amazed by what folks say here. It's almost like they forget I'm working back at the grill."

"I need to know what you've heard," I said. "I'm not about to accuse anybody of murder without facts, but I do need to know where to look. You mentioned the mayor and Kendra Williams. Do you have any other suspects in mind?"

She bit her lip, so I added, "Besides the obvious ones like Hannah and David? I'm not even going to consider either one of them at the moment."

She didn't look all that happy when she said, "It's possible, though. You have to admit that."

What was Shelly getting at? "Do you know something I don't?"

"Knowing and proving are two different things, aren't they? Each one of them had motive enough, didn't they?"

I stabbed a bite of pancake and ate it before I trusted myself to speak. "I'm not going to even think about that possibility. Let the sheriff worry about them. I want to talk to people Hodges won't. Come on, Shelly, if you know something, tell me."

She hesitated, then said, "As soon as I heard about the murder, I started thinking about who might have killed Richard Atkins. Besides the four people we've talked about, I know of two other folks who might have hated him enough to kill him."

I waited ten seconds, then asked, "Who are they?"

She lowered her voice. "Remember, you never heard this from me, okay?"

"I promise I won't tell anyone where I got my information." What more did she want, a blood oath?

"Richard was seeing someone on the side while he was married to Hannah," she said softly. "When he took off, he left her high and dry, too."

"Who was it?"

"She has a shop near yours."

97

"Kendra was sleeping with him, too?" I couldn't imagine that particular union, and I would have paid good money to get the thought excised from my mind.

"No, I'm talking about Rose Nygren."

I was nearly as surprised by that name as I would have been by Kendra's. "Timid little Rose, of Rose Colored Glasses? Are you sure?"

"She hasn't always been that soft-spoken," Shelly said. "I never caught them doing anything, but a few folks around town saw some things that made me wonder. I remember after Richard left, Rose was nearly inconsolable."

That would definitely bear looking into. "Who else? There wasn't another woman, was there? How did the man find the energy, let alone the time?"

"No, it was just Hannah and Rose; at least those were the only two I was aware of."

"So, who else would want him dead?"

Shelly frowned, then said, "If you repeat this, I'll deny it and call you a liar, okay? It's not something I want to talk to you about anyway."

"I already gave you my word," I said. "What more can I give you to convince you?"

She appeared to think about it a few

seconds, then nodded. "You should talk to the man Rose was seeing at the time. He never forgave her for the affair, and I doubt he'd have given up his grudge against Richard, even after all these years. Rose was the love of his life, and he never forgot her, even if he couldn't get past what she'd done."

"All you need to do now is give me a name," I said.

"I will, but you're not going to like it. I hate to have to be the one to tell you this, but it's your uncle Don."

"What? I'm not one of his biggest fans, but I can't imagine Don killing anyone, can you?" Don Rutledge was my mother's youngest brother, a slim, hard-eyed man with a fiery temper and such a generally bad demeanor that he was an outcast at every family reunion. He'd gotten drunk at my wedding, dove headfirst into the cake, and somehow managed to knock off my mother's wig in the process. I'd stopped calling him "uncle" years ago, and I avoided him whenever I could, though we lived less than twenty miles apart. Still, I'd have to talk to Don, even if it meant dragging up a past I'd just as soon forget. I loved David and Hannah more than a disenfranchised uncle. Some folks cared only about blood relations. What mattered to me was what was in someone's heart. Hannah and her son were more a part of my real family than Don would ever be.

"Is there anybody else I should talk to?" I asked.

"How about a psychiatrist? Are you really going to try to solve this murder on your own?"

"I don't have much choice, do I?"

Shelly stared hard at me. "You could always butt out and let the sheriff do his job."

"I suppose I could, but I'm not going to. Whose side are you on, anyway?"

She touched my hand lightly. "Yours, always yours. You shouldn't even have to ask."

I slid a ten under my plate and started to get up.

"Hey, that's too much," Shelly said.

"Think of it as a nice tip."

"I don't think so," she said as she made change. I took the money and jammed it into my purse.

Shelly frowned. "Do you mean I don't get any tip at all now?"

"Make up your mind," I said as I slid a single under my plate. "If you think of anything else, call me, okay?"

She cracked the single in her hands. "With

tips like this, I'll be burning up the phone lines hoping for more."

I left her place and glanced at my watch. I'd tarried much too long over my meal, and if I was going to make my standing date with Hannah, I'd have to rush to get to In the Grounds.

I needn't have bothered. Hannah never showed up, though I lingered over my coffee much longer than I should have. After all, I had people I needed to see before it was time to open Fire at Will. I hated the thought of closing up shop during the workday again, but with David absent, and without any idea of when the boy was coming back, I knew I might not have much choice. Out of my list of suspects, Don was the one I least wanted to speak to, so I put him at the head of my roll. I'd discovered long ago that the more I dreaded doing something, the quicker I needed to do it. Otherwise it would linger over me like a black rain cloud until I took care of it.

I got into my Intrigue and headed toward Autumn Landing. It was time to see if Don might have had something to do with Richard Atkins's murder.

I was half hoping my uncle wouldn't be

home as I drove to his house. I would have rather had a sleepover with Kendra Williams than talk to Don.

He kept a nice yard and house, I had to say that for the man. The grass was manicured, the shrubs were precisely trimmed, and the paint on the house wasn't more than six months old. It was as clean and sterile as a magazine layout, and I knew the inside would be just as stark. I was idling in his driveway, trying to work up the nerve to approach the house, when his front door opened.

It was a pretty unusual welcome, since he had a shotgun in his hands.

"Hi, Don," I said through my open window.

"Carolyn, what are you doing here?"

"Trying not to get shot at the moment. Do you mind lowering that thing? I'm looking for some information." I wasn't all that comfortable staring down those double barrels.

"What? Sorry," he said as the gun muzzle dipped. "I thought you were somebody else."

"Care to give me a hint who you're waiting for?" I asked as I got out of my car, wondering who my uncle had ticked off recently.

"The government says I owe more on my taxes than I do. We've been having a little disagreement about it."

"So you greet federal agents with a shotgun?"

He grinned. "It's not like it's loaded." He pulled the trigger, and I heard a thunderous boom as the turf at his feet exploded with the impact of the pellets.

"I thought I took those shells out," he said calmly as he breached the gun and pulled out two shells, one spent and one fresh. "Sorry about that."

"No problem," I said, my knees feeling a little weak. I expected the neighbors to come pouring out of their homes to see what had happened, but not a door opened, though I saw a few curtains fluttering without the aid of a breeze.

"Blast it all," he said, staring at the ground where the buckshot had gone into the dirt. "I hate that that happened."

"No one was hurt, but you should be more careful," I said.

"You're telling me. Do you have any idea how long it took me to get this turf just right? I'm going to have to start all over on this patch. It's ruined."

So much for my uncle's familial concern.

"I'll leave you to it, then," I said as I

started to get back into my car.

"You never said why you came by," he said.

"Forget it." The last thing I wanted to do was get on this lunatic's bad side. If anything, he'd gotten worse over the years.

"That's the problem," he said. "I can't just let it go."

I didn't want him stalking me. "I came to talk to you about Richard Atkins."

He frowned, then said, "There's a name I'd just about forgotten." He twisted the ring on his right pinky, a bright green stone of adventurine mounted on gold. The twisting appeared to be a nervous habit, and I wondered what he had to be concerned about. "What happened, did he finally get himself killed?"

"Now why do you ask that?"

"It was bound to happen sooner or later, the way the man acted. Don't tell me it happened in Maple Ridge?"

"In back of my house, actually. I understand you weren't his biggest fan."

My uncle grinned, but there was not an ounce of warmth in it. "He took something of mine, something I didn't want to let go."

"So it's true? You actually went out with Rose Nygren once upon a time?"

Don looked shocked by the suggestion.

"Now where on God's green earth did you hear that?"

"A friend told me," I admitted.

"Well, your friend lied to you. My relationship with Rose was a little different than that. She was a good friend of mine, and Richard ruined her."

"It's obvious you didn't care for the man, but did you hate him enough to kill him?" I asked softly.

He raised the shotgun in the air again, and although I knew it was unloaded, I still felt uneasy having it pointed straight at me. "You didn't chuck that pottery store of yours and join the police force, did you?"

"No, I still run my shop." I certainly wasn't going to say "Fire at Will" while he was holding a gun on me.

"Then why are you snooping around?"

I wondered what our front-yard conversation must look like to Don's neighbors, but I doubted any of them would try to rescue me. "Hannah Atkins is my best friend, and her son, David, works for me. I'm not going to let the sheriff's suspicions settle on either one of them."

"So you'd rather pin it on family than have it pinned on your friends, is that it?" I swear, I could see his finger tighten on the trigger. The gun *was* unloaded, wasn't it? I was growing less sure with every passing second.

"I just want to find out the truth," I said, attempting to keep my voice from quivering.

"The truth's a slippery thing, Carolyn," he said.

I was still trying to figure out how to reply to that when he said, "Leave Rose out of this. Do you understand me?"

"Are you actually threatening me, Don?"

"It's Uncle Don, if you don't mind. And no, I'm not threatening my sister's kid." He stared long and hard at me, then added, "But I am warning her. There are a dozen other folks around town who wanted to see that man dead. Go try looking at them."

"Anybody in particular you have in mind?"

"Start at the mayor's office and work your way down."

It was clear I wasn't going to get anything else out of him. I started to get back into my car for the second time, and managed to shut the door before he spoke. "Where are you going?"

"I've got a business to run," I said. "Remember?"

"Just as long as it's not mine." He held the shotgun firm in his grip. "Heed my words, Carolyn."

I managed to muster a weak grin in reply before backing out of the driveway.

As I drove away, I felt an itching in the back of my neck where the pellets would hit if my uncled fired, and it didn't go away entirely until I was out of sight of his house. Would Don Rutledge have actually shot me? On purpose, I mean. I hadn't been worried until Rose Nygren's name had come up. At that moment, I honestly believed that my uncle was capable of just about anything.

But I wasn't going to let that deter me. In fact, I was going to visit Rose before it was time to open Fire at Will. Maybe I could get the truth out of her. At the very least, I doubted she'd take a shot at me.

Rose was playing with her front window display when I walked up to Rose Colored Glasses. I'd always enjoyed a clever name, and Rose's was perfect, even without knowing the proprietress's name. I could see through the glass that Rose's red hair was pulled back into a ponytail. I tapped on the display window and she jerked up, so startled that she dropped a lovely red stained glass hot-air balloon. It shattered on the brick floor, and I felt sick at the sight of the broken pieces.

I walked inside and said, "Rose, I'm so

sorry. I didn't mean to startle you."

"It's fine, Carolyn. It happens more than you'd imagine." As always, her lilting voice was almost a whisper.

"Have you ever thought about carpeting the place?" I said. The bricks had to be torture on stained glass.

"Carpet is so sterile," she said. "I love the textures of the bricks, and if it means I lose a piece now and then, so be it."

"I'll be happy to pay for it," I said, reaching for my purse.

"Nonsense. It was an accident. You weren't even the one who dropped it."

"No, but I caused it as surely as if I'd knocked it out of your hands. How much is it? I insist."

"They're thirty-nine dollars," Rose said almost apologetically. Thirty-nine bucks for that? I was in the wrong business. I counted out four tens from my wallet and handed them to her.

She wouldn't take the money. Instead, she said, "At least let me sell it to you at cost."

"No," I said, despite being tempted. "I robbed you of a sale, so I won't hear of it."

She accepted the money, folding it up and putting it into her apron, rather than the register, and I wondered if my money would ever see her till. I thought about the single I had coming back to me in change, but decided not to make an issue of it.

"Since I'm here, I'd like to talk to you," I said. At least my forty dollars might grant me an interview.

She glanced at her watch. "I've got a few minutes. What's it about?"

She started to rearrange the window display now that one of her hot-air balloons was gone, but I couldn't afford to pay any more breakage fees. "May we sit for a moment?"

She reluctantly agreed, and we moved over to her sales counter where she had two chairs poised nearby. "What would you like to talk about?"

"It's about what happened last night," I said.

"Why? What happened?"

"You mean you haven't heard?" I asked. I'd been sure some branch of the Maple Ridge grapevine would have reached her by now, but evidently I was mistaken.

"I went to bed early last night, and I haven't spoken to anyone this morning. What is it, Carolyn?"

"Somebody killed Richard Atkins in my backyard last night."

I was watching her face, but she showed no reaction at all. It was as if she already knew, but that didn't match what she'd just told me.

"So, it finally happened," she said after a moment.

"You don't seem all that surprised, if you don't mind me saying so," I said.

"I'm long past letting anything catch me off guard," she said. "If you'll excuse me, there's someone I need to call before I open."

I hoped it wasn't Don. "Do me a favor, don't tell anyone I told you, okay?"

"Why not? Is it some kind of secret? You did call the police, didn't you?"

"Of course I did," I said as I stood. "I just don't want anyone to think I'm being cold, talking about it like this."

"Certainly. Now I really must make that call."

I walked outside, and Rose locked the door behind me. I gave her twenty seconds, then I took out my cell phone and dialed my uncle's telephone number. It was busy. Perhaps it was just a coincidence, but I doubted it. Until I knew different, I was going to assume that Rose had phoned my uncle. Why would she call him, though? To tell him the news, or perhaps to thank him? I wasn't sure how I could find out, but I didn't want to attract unwanted attention by standing in front of Rose's locked shop hitting redial every seven seconds. I headed toward Fire at Will.

As I walked past Hattie's Attic, I didn't even think about Kendra Williams, I was so focused on wondering what my uncle and Rose were up to. Kendra wasn't about to let me just pass her by, though.

"How dreadful for you." I didn't need to see the faded muumuu to realize Kendra was talking to me.

"I could say the same thing to you," I said.

She looked taken aback by my comment. "Whatever are you talking about? Are you in some kind of shock after finding that dreadful man's body?"

I leaned in toward her, something that made her uncomfortable, if the sour expression on her face was any indication. "I'm fine, but I wonder if you are."

"You're talking nonsense," she said, taking two steps back toward the safety of her shop.

"Am I?" I followed her, matching my steps with hers.

"I've got to go." She was in full retreat now.

"I'm right behind you." It was nice unnerving her for a change, but it wasn't going to get me any information. Before she could escape inside Hattie's Attic, I said, "You must be relieved the man's dead."

"Carolyn, I'm willing to make allowances, given what happened last night, but I won't stand here and be insulted like this."

"Would you rather go inside and sit down?" I asked. "We can do this in your shop, if you'd like."

"I don't know what you think you're doing, but you're not going to browbeat me in front of my own place of business. I'll thank you not to come back until you can act normally."

"No promises there, Kendra," I said.

She nearly ran inside, and I waited to hear the dead bolt slam shut, but apparently even my behavior wasn't enough to keep her from losing a sale. Kendra was jumpy, but I didn't know if it was because of what had happened the night before, or the way I was acting. No matter how much joy it gave me to see her off balance, I couldn't afford to alienate her by applying too much pressure.

I walked over to Fire at Will and unlocked the front door. A part of me was hoping David would greet me as I walked in, but there was no sign of him — until I walked in back. There I saw my comforter spread out on the couch and some wrappers from a convenience store on the floor beside it. It had to have been David. While I would have normally fussed at him for not cleaning up his messes or warning me he'd be camping out in my back room, I didn't care. At least it meant he was still all right.

I picked up the phone next to the couch and had started to dial Hannah's number when I heard tapping on the front door. I still had two minutes until I officially opened. Whoever was out there would just have to wait. Hannah's phone kicked me straight to voice mail. I said quickly, "It's Carolyn. Call me as soon as you get this."

I hung up and looked out the front window. It was my dapper elderly gentleman from the day before. He was back to finish up his house. I vowed not to lift a finger, to make him do the glazing himself.

After turning on the lights, I unlocked the door, and he bolted in past me. "Sorry to be so impatient," he said, "but I just couldn't wait."

"That's fine," I said. "Let's see how it turned out." I led him back to the kiln and opened the top. It was cool enough to reach in and pull out his clay house. "There it is," I said.

"It's all pink," he said, obviously a little disappointed in the hue of the building.

"Remember, we're going to paint it next,

so it won't stay that way."

He looked over my shoulder and saw the nearly full kiln. I said, "I had a few other things to add at the last second. Things fire more uniformly if it's a full load."

"Rightly so," he said. "You don't want to waste the electricity either. It is electric, isn't it? I don't see any gas lines."

"I have a gas kiln at home," I said, "but we use electric ones here." I wasn't going to finish unloading the kiln with him standing there, but he must have spotted the house I'd made after I retrieved his. "Did you do another one?"

"It was fun, so I decided to make one, too," I admitted.

He looked delighted. "Well, bring it out. Let's see what you've come up with."

He took my decidedly more eccentric house and studied it as carefully as if it were an architectural rendition instead of a flight of my whimsy.

Finally, he declared, "It's perfect. You must glaze yours along beside me."

He was paying for the privilege, and besides, it sounded like fun. "Let's pick out some colors then. Do you have anything special in mind?"

"Of course. The exterior should be a gray pristine enough to represent a weathered shade of white, while the windows should be painted forest green. The roof needs to be a brown, the tint of autumn loam, and the chimney should be faded red."

Okay, that was a little more specific than I'd been looking for, but he certainly gave me a good set of guidelines. I started pulling out paints and mixing to get the shades he was after. He looked at the palette with obvious disappointment. "My, those are rather muted, aren't they?"

"Wait until they go through the kiln. I think you'll be happy with the colors I've come up with."

He frowned at the paints as if he didn't believe me.

"Look, it's as easy as this," I said as I grabbed a brush and started laying on the main body tint.

When I finished, I handed him the brush. At least I tried to. He refused, saying, "I just don't have the touch you seem to. Would you mind?"

It was beginning to look as though this project was all mine, but I didn't have any other customers, and he had paid for the privilege with his firing fee the day before. Besides, I enjoyed painting pieces. "How's that look?" I asked when I'd finished.

"Rather bland, I'm afraid."

"I'll tell you what, if you're still disappointed after it's been fired, I'll refund your fee. How's that sound?" What was I saying? I'd already spent some of the hundred he'd given me, and here I was offering a full refund. I suddenly had more at stake than I had intended.

"I couldn't do that," he said. "Will you be firing again tonight?"

I didn't want to, since there weren't enough pieces to make it worth the expense, but I was feeling bad about taking so much before. "For you, I'll run it through tonight."

"Excellent," he said. "Do you mind if I watch you decorate yours? I'm in a bit of a rush, but I'd love to see your preliminary step."

"Why not?" I chose a rusty red and dusty blue to decorate my cottage, then added some ivy outside as an afterthought.

"What was that last bit?"

"I thought some ivy would look good crawling up the outside of my place," I said. "Would you like some on yours?"

"No, there's no ivy on mine," he said resolutely. I had to give him credit. He had the most specific imagination I'd ever run into. "Same time tomorrow?"

"I'll have it ready for you," I said.

I don't know if I would have taken another

hundred if he'd offered it, but it didn't matter, because he didn't. Where was Hannah, and why wasn't she calling me back? I thought about trying her again, but I knew she was extraordinarily conscientious about returning her calls. I'd give her more time. In the meantime, I decided I might as well fill up that kiln, so I decorated another batch of my ornaments that I'd bisque fired the week before. I enjoyed doing them, letting my imagination run wild with the colors and designs. After I'd stacked the kiln, I decided to go ahead with the firing.

It was a good morning's worth of work, but I was increasingly uneasy about how much time had passed without any word from David or Hannah.

I was just about to pick up the phone and try her again when I saw Hannah outside rushing toward my front door. From the expression on her face, I could tell something had gone horribly wrong.

CHAPTER 6

"I don't know what I'm going to do," my best friend said as she nearly collapsed in my arms. "David never came home last night."

If Hannah had gotten even an hour's worth of sleep the night before, she certainly didn't look it. Normally stylish and sharply dressed, she appeared to have slept in the suit she was wearing; uncharacteristic bags shadowed her eyes. Her hair, usually so well tamed, was frazzled and frayed, no doubt much like the woman's spirit.

"From the way I found my back room this morning, I'm guessing he stayed here," I said as I held her.

She jerked away from me as if I were on fire. "He was here? Why didn't you tell me?"

"I tried to call you this morning when I got in, but you weren't answering your phone. I left you a message."

"Oh, no," she said as she pulled her cell

phone out of her purse. "I forgot to charge it. The battery's dead. What if David's been trying to reach me?"

"Let me see it." One glance was all it took. "I have the exact same phone you do. Take my battery. I charged it last night."

"That will leave you without a phone, though."

I fumbled with the back of my cell phone, took out the battery, and pushed it at her. "If anybody needs me, they can call me here. Your need is a little more urgent than mine."

We swapped batteries, and I plugged my phone into its charger. I kept one charger at home and another at the shop, since I was always forgetting to plug in my cell phone, or turn it off, for that matter.

She checked her voice-mail messages and had four waiting, but only one of them mattered to her. It was from David, and after she listened to it once, she handed it to me.

"Mom, I'm okay. I can't come home. I'm in . . . ," and then the message died. What had he been trying to add? Was he in love? In trouble? In England? In jail? The dead tone of his voice didn't betray much additional information.

"What does it mean?" Hannah asked.

"It means he was okay last night, and

probably this morning, too. That's got to count for something."

"Carolyn, I need to know."

"I know you do, but there's nothing you can do about it right now, is there? If you can think of anything constructive to do, I'll help. You know I will."

She frowned at me, then started to cry. As I held my distraught friend, I tried to imagine how I would feel if one of my sons were in trouble. I didn't have to think about it for very long. Without a doubt, I would be ready to rip the world apart to find him.

"I don't know what to do," she stammered out.

"I know. It's okay, Hannah. He's going to be all right."

She blew her nose into a tissue. "I wish I could be as sure about it as you are."

"It's easier for me," I said as I handed her the whole box. "It's not my son we're talking about."

"He thinks of you as his other mother. You know that, don't you?" She wiped at her tears, but the tissues were no match.

"I love him, too. Listen to me. David is smart, he's resourceful, and he's got a good head on his shoulders. He's going to be all right."

"Doesn't he know he's just making things

worse hiding like this? The sheriff's certain he killed Richard. That's why he keeps hounding me."

I picked up a mug from the sale table that someone had painted, paid for, then abandoned. It was an ugly little thing, but at least it gave me something to do with my hands. "Does the sheriff suspect anyone else?"

"Besides me, you mean?" She rolled her eyes. "He's already determined that if David didn't kill his father, I did it myself. I'm not afraid to admit that I had more reason than most to do it, but I didn't, and David didn't, either. He wouldn't. He couldn't. I wouldn't believe it if he himself told me he'd done it."

"Of course he didn't do it," I said, trying to soothe her. I hadn't lied. I did love David, but that didn't mean I was blind to his faults. He had a temper sometimes, and it was quick and sharp and strong when it reared its head. If he were in one of his moods, and Richard's sudden reappearance had triggered it, I wasn't sure what he might do.

"I can't stay here," Hannah said, "but I just had to come see you."

"If I hear from David, I'll call you, or make him do it himself. Don't worry. What am I saying, of course you're going to worry.

If it helps, I'll be worrying, too."

"It does," she said as she squeezed my hand. "You're a true friend."

"So are you," I said.

"I've got to go," she said, fighting back another jag of tears. "You'll call me. You promise?"

"I swear. Where are you going?"

She thought about it a minute, then said, "I need to be home. It's the first place David will look for me."

And the first place the sheriff would expect, too, I thought. But I didn't say it aloud. Hannah didn't need to hear that from me, or anyone else.

After she left, I was trying to decide what I should do when the front door chimed. In walked Butch, followed by Jenna and Sandy. The Firing Squad had come to help me in my hour of need, and I knew if Martha hadn't had a house full of sick children, she'd be right there with them.

I just wished I knew some way they could help.

"We need a course of action," Jenna said as we gathered in back. I stood in the doorway where I could keep an eye on the front, just in case a customer happened to wander in. Hey, stranger things had happened.

"Where could David be?" Sandy asked.

"That's the question, isn't it?" I asked. "Folks, I appreciate you coming by, but I don't know what any of us can do."

Butch put a big paw on my shoulder. "That's not like you, Carolyn. Finding that body must have been tough on you."

"I do seem to stumble across more than my share," I admitted. "But that's not why I'm so pessimistic. David was shattered when Richard told him he was his father. You should have seen his face." I didn't want to say it, but I had to tell these people what they might be dealing with. "He wasn't himself. I don't know what he might have done."

Butch squeezed my shoulder, and I tried not to wince. "Carolyn, in his worst hour, David's not a killer. But the kid has to be pretty shook up by what happened. Finding, then losing your old man in a span of a few hours would be hard on anyone." He released his grip, and I tried to hold in my relief.

Jenna said, "Let's find him. I'm sure we can do it if we just use our heads."

"If it helps, I'm pretty sure he spent last night on my couch," I said.

"He was at your house?" Sandy asked. "Why didn't you tell us that from the start?"

"Not my couch at home," I said as I pointed to the one in back of the shop. "He slept there, and from the look of the way he left things, he was in a rush when he took off."

Butch walked around the couch as if it were a fascinating artifact instead of the discount sofa it really was. "It looks clean to me."

"That's because I just couldn't leave it like it was."

"Where's the trash bag?" he asked.

"I tossed it in the Dumpster in back. You're not going to dig through my trash, are you?"

"I've done a lot worse in my life," he said with a grin. "I'll be back shortly."

I appreciated their help, truly I did, but there was no way I was going to let him sort through my rubbish in my shop. "Don't bring that bag back in here. Please."

Butch nodded. "You got it."

At least he was abandoning that plan. Or so I thought.

"I'll do it out back. No offense, but I need room to work anyway."

Was he serious? "Go on, then."

"Don't worry, Carolyn, I'll clean up after myself. Where are your spare trash bags?"

I pointed to the bathroom. "I keep some

back there."

He grabbed a few bags, then headed out back. As he reached the rear entrance, he stopped and asked, "Anyone care to join me? No? Okay, suit yourselves."

When the door shut, I asked Jenna and Sandy, "Has he lost his mind?"

"No, the police do it all the time," Jenna said, "a fact that's not lost on our friend, I'm sure. Let's see if we can come up with something ourselves while we're waiting for Butch."

Sandy walked over and picked up the telephone. "Have you used this phone since you came in this morning?"

I remembered my frantic telephone call to Hannah when I'd first found the mess. "Sorry, I called Hannah this morning."

"That's all right, how could you know? Redial would have been nice, but there's got to be something here." She started digging under the cushions of the sofa.

"If you're looking for spare change, I've got some in my purse," I said.

"I'm looking for clues," she said.

Jenna smiled. "I thought the Internet was your specialty."

"Hey, a gal's got to branch out sometimes, doesn't she? What's this?" Sandy held out a wadded-up sheet of paper and started to open it as Jenna and I approached so we could see it as well.

We looked at the paper and saw the numbers 06-07-91 written on it in what was unmistakably David's handwriting. Sandy frowned at it and said, "What is it, some kind of combination? I wonder if it's to a safe."

"Yes, David is so rich he needs a safe to keep his money in," I said dryly.

"It could be a birthday," Jenna suggested. I glanced at a calendar I got from my glaze supplier. "It doesn't mean anything to me."

"It's got to mean something to him, though," Sandy said, too proud of her discovery to allow any dispute.

"Sandy, we have no idea how long that's been there. David could have left it months ago."

"You haven't had the couch that long," Jenna said.

That was true. I'd been forced to replace the old one when I'd discovered something about it that I preferred to forget. I'd had the new one for only a few weeks. "That still doesn't mean he left it last night."

Butch came back in holding a soiled piece of paper.

"What did you find?" I asked him.

"This was torn from a pad. There's an

126

impression of something, but I can't see what it is. Hand me a pencil."

I gave him one from the counter near where I was standing, and he rubbed the edge of the graphite along the sheet. After he'd done that to his satisfaction, Butch held the paper up to the light and read, "I think it's a six up front. Let's see, that looks like it might be a one right there."

"Could it be a seven, by any chance?" Jenna asked, trying to suppress her grin.

"Hang on, let me see. Yes, I think you're right. It does look like a seven. Now how in the world did you know that?"

Jenna grabbed Sandy's paper and handed it to him. "We found the original. Or Sandy did, I should say."

The librarian was grinning broadly.

"You're quite proud of that, aren't you?" I asked.

"That's not why I'm smiling. The paper Butch has proves that David wrote this last night. It's got to mean something."

"I suppose you're right," I admitted.

"It has to be."

Jenna said, "But we still don't know what it opens. Or if it even opens anything."

I looked at Butch, and he was frowning.

I couldn't have that. "You gave us valuable confirmation. Don't look so glum."

"That's not it," he said. "This could be something else."

"We're listening, if you have any ideas," I said.

"What if it belongs to a security system for someone's business, or even their house?"

Jenna said, "Surely you're not accusing David of being a burglar, are you?"

"No," Butch said patiently. "He doesn't have the skills for it. But if we knew where it matched, it might tell us where he is right now."

Sandy asked, "What kind of skills do you need to steal?" Her tone of voice wasn't accusatory. She was obviously fascinated by the subject, but we didn't have time for one of Butch's discourses on the art of thievery.

"Never mind that right now," I said. "There can't be that many homes in Maple Ridge that require a security code, can there?"

"You'd be surprised," Butch said. "There are more around here than you'd think."

"I'd really love to know how a reformed thief would know that," Jenna said sternly.

"I can't help what I notice," Butch said. "Once you've trained your eyes to look for certain things, you can't just ignore those observations, even if the information isn't pertinent anymore."

"Would you two please hush?" I asked. "I'm thinking."

I dared Butch to say something about my scolding, but he kept silent. Why on earth would David have a security combination for someone's house? Where would he get one? Then I remembered what his girlfriend did for a living.

As I reached for the telephone, I said, "I've got to make a call."

"Who are you calling?" Sandy asked.

"Annie Gregg. Hush, it's ringing."

After seven rings, she picked up. "AG A1," she answered.

I knew that was the name of her cleaning business. It was clever, catchy, and had the distinct advantage of being listed first in the Yellow Pages.

"Annie, it's Carolyn."

She sighed deeply and then said, "Carolyn, I haven't seen David since yesterday morning."

"But have you spoken with him?" I asked. "Perhaps long enough to give him the security code for someone's home who happens to be out of town, maybe a client who is trusting you to care for their property while they're away?"

Okay, perhaps I was being a little heavy-

129

handed, but I needed to find David before he got into any more trouble. I added, "You're not helping him, Annie, despite what you might think."

In a voice that was nearly a whisper, she said, "He made me promise not to tell. I talked to him this morning."

"I won't say anything," I said as reassuringly as I could. "Where is he, Annie? I need to know. It's for his own good."

"I can't tell you anything," she said after a long pause.

"Could you at least give me a hint? I found the security code here at the shop. That is what 06-07-91 means, isn't it?"

"Yes," she admitted. Again in a near whisper, she added, "Look up and you might see him."

"What?"

"I won't say anything more, Carolyn. Good-bye." She hung up before I could say another word.

Had the dear child spent too much time breathing in cleaning fluid fumes? Look up. Was she kidding me? And then I realized what she had to have meant. There was one place, a stately mansion indeed, that looked down on all of Maple Ridge, and I'd been there a few times myself.

Tamra Gentry was in New York the last

I'd heard. Her estate on the mountainside would be the perfect place for David to hide out.

"Let's go," I said as I started for the front door.

Butch said, "Let me lock up the back entrance. You can't trust people these days. Carolyn, you really should update your security system around here."

"What are they going to take, a few bags of clay and some glaze? I'll risk it."

"Those kilns might be expensive to replace."

"Enough of this. Where exactly are we going?" Jenna asked.

"Tamra Gentry's place. I've got a pretty good idea that's where David is hiding out."

"Let's go," Sandy said.

"Don't you have to work? I don't want to get you in trouble with Corki."

"I took a sick day as soon as I heard about David. Do you honestly think I could work and not help him? He's my friend, too, Carolyn."

I hugged her quickly. "I knew there was a reason I was so fond of you."

"Hey, I'm coming, too," Butch protested.

I hugged him as well, then turned to Jenna. "How about you?"

"I'm coming, but we can skip the embrace," she said. "Are you all quite ready?"

"Absolutely." I grabbed the "Closed" sign and hung it in the door without another thought. If it meant I lost some business, so be it. David took precedence over everything else at the moment.

Butch said, "I'll drive," and none of us argued with him. His Cadillac had plenty of room, and if there was an option he didn't have on it, it was purely by accident.

As we drove up the steep, winding road to Tamra's place, I thought about what I would say to David. Should I scold him for running away like he had? For that matter, should I even bring up his father's death? I'd have to figure it out on the fly.

The leaves of a hundred maple trees obscured the drive, but I could still see Tamra's place through gaps in the canopy. It truly was a stately place, a three-story colonial with massive white columns in front that loomed over all of Maple Ridge.

It was impossible to tell if Tamra, or anyone else, for that matter, was in residence. Had I guessed right? David didn't have to come out if he didn't want to. Although I had the security code, I suddenly realized that I didn't have a key, something I had neglected to ask Annie about.

Butch parked in front of the house.

I reached for my phone, but couldn't find it anywhere in my purse. Then I remembered that it was still in the charger at the shop, the good battery now on Hannah's phone. "Can I borrow one of your cell phones? I need to make one more call."

"We're already here," Sandy said. "Let's just go in."

"I have the code, but we still need a key," I said.

"Sorry, I forgot all about that."

I shouldn't have snapped at the poor girl, since I'd forgotten that myself. I smiled. "To be honest with you, so did I, until thirty seconds ago."

"We don't necessarily need a key," Butch said in a soft voice. Before Jenna could protest, he added, "I'm just saying."

"Make your call, Carolyn," Jenna said as she handed me her cell phone.

This time, Annie picked up on the first ring. I said, "Annie, it's me again. I know there must be a key hidden out here somewhere. That's the way Tamra is." It was a guess, but I thought it was a good one.

"Where are you?" I detected a little bit of fright in her voice, as if she'd said too much earlier.

"I know David's at Tamra's, but I'm afraid if I ring the bell, he'll try to run again."

That wasn't really true; I had no idea how David would react, but I needed this girl's help.

"I want the best for him, too. Surely you know that."

Was she crying? I wasn't sure, and the sound stopped nearly as soon as it had started. Finally, she said, "Look under one of the columns. There's a bit of detail work hiding the key. You have to push on a slight paint smear and it opens up."

"You've got to be kidding me," I said as I got out of the car in search of this secret hiding place. It was obvious the others wanted to know what I was up to, but to their credit, they followed me in relative silence. I studied each column's base and couldn't see a thing that looked out of the ordinary. "It's not here."

"The key's gone? David must still have it," she said.

"No, I'm talking about the paint smudge. It's simply not on any of the bases."

"Are you sure you're looking carefully enough?" Annie asked.

"I can see a smudge without my glasses," I said abruptly. "Which column is it in? Do you remember?"

She paused, then said, "I think it's on the right side. It's not the key I use, but Tamra told me about it in case I lost mine."

"I started from the left," I said, "but I'll keep looking."

"I'm sorry, I'm just not myself."

"It's all right, dear," I said. "I can't imagine how hard this is for you."

"Thanks for being so understanding, Carolyn."

"That's what I do," I said. "I'm looking, but I still don't see it." The others must have thought I'd lost my mind, but they didn't say a word as I stared intently at the column bases. I explained what I was looking for, then Butch got down on his hands and knees and started studying one himself. He frowned a second, then poked a spot I'd missed. To my surprise, a small door opened, and there, inside the base, lay a key.

"We found it," I said.

"We? You didn't bring the police with you, did you?"

"Of course not, Annie. Now I've got to go."

"You won't tell him I told you, will you?"

"I promise," I said, and then I hung up. I stared at Butch as he handed me the key. "How on earth did you know to do that?"

"It was pretty obvious, wasn't it?" he said, trying not to sound too smug.

"Maybe to you," I said.

I took the key and approached the door.

Jenna put a hand on my arm before I could try it. "Are you sure we shouldn't ring the bell first? We might frighten him off if we just barge in."

"I'll call out his name as soon as we get inside," I said.

I slipped the key into the lock and gently turned the knob. As I slowly pushed the door inward, I saw a handgun leveled at my chest, and David's finger nearly white on the trigger.

CHAPTER 7

"Would you mind pointing that somewhere else?" I asked David as calmly as I could manage. This was the second weapon pointed at me today, definitely a trend I wanted to discourage.

"Sorry, I didn't know it was you," David said as he lowered the gun to his side.

Butch walked past me and took it from David's grasp. "You should never point one of these things at somebody unless you're willing to use it," he said. "And before you can do that, you've got to take the safety off, like this." He moved a small lever and handed the gun back to David. "Now it's ready to shoot."

"Give me that," Jenna snapped, and David handed it to her. She put it gingerly in Butch's hands. "Put the safety back on, unload it, and then, David, put it back where you found it."

"Fine," he said. "What are you all doing

here? Annie told you where I was hiding, didn't she?"

I wasn't about to tell on her. "It wasn't that difficult to figure out," I said before the others could stop me. "You left the security code wadded up on the couch. The alarm's not set right now, is it? We wouldn't want the sheriff showing up." I added with a frown, "Nice housekeeping in the shop, by the way."

"Sorry," he said sheepishly. "I was in a bit of a rush to get out of there. That still doesn't explain how you knew to come here. Annie must have told you where I was, and where to find the key."

Butch grinned at him. "I used to be a crook, remember?" The man was taking a page from my book, lying convincingly by telling the truth. There was an art to it, one Butch had obviously mastered long ago.

"I can't even hide right," David said miserably.

Sandy approached him. "Do you know about your father?"

David's head shot up. "That man is not my father. He walked out on my mother before I was born. What was he thinking, coming back here after all this time?"

Jenna asked softly, "You know he's dead, don't you?"

David looked wildly at us. "I didn't kill him!"

"We believe you, but if you didn't have anything to do with his death, why are you hiding?" I had to know.

David looked at me as if I'd lost my mind. "You're the one who keeps saying what a fool Sheriff Hodges is. If I show my face, he'll arrest me for sure."

"You don't know that," I said. "And I never said Hodges was a fool. He's a lot of things, including lazy, but he's not stupid, David. You're just making things worse for yourself hiding like this."

"I can't just walk into town now, can I?"

Butch stroked his chin. "Why not? You haven't done anything." He paused for a few seconds, then smiled. "In fact, that's exactly what you should do. David, you need to head back into town with us, go to work with Carolyn at the shop, and call your mother. She's worried sick about you."

David looked ill at the suggestion. "I tried to call her this morning, but she wasn't picking up her cell phone."

"That's because she left her phone on all night so you could call her," I said. "I agree with Butch's plan, with one change. You'll borrow Jenna's cell phone and call your mother on the way down the hill."

"So you honestly think I should just act like nothing's happened? What about you, Jenna? What do you think?"

"I have to agree with them, David. If you haven't done anything wrong, there's no reason to hide. Don't forget, I was a lawyer long before I was a judge. I'll stay at the shop for the rest of the day, in case you have any trouble with the sheriff."

"You'd do that for me?"

"Of course I would," she said. "We will all do whatever we can to help you. We're here, aren't we? Now let's forget this foolishness and go to Fire at Will."

He looked relieved that we'd stepped in. At least until Jenna handed him her phone. "Call your mother," Jenna and I said in unison.

He nodded reluctantly. "Fine. Can I call her before we go, though? I'd like a little privacy."

"Need I remind you all that we're here unlawfully?" Jenna asked. "It wouldn't do to tarry."

"I won't be long. I promise," David said as he walked back to the bedroom area.

The four of us waited in the living room, and I saw Sandy frowning. "Is that what I think it is? No, it couldn't be."

She was admiring the Monet I'd spotted

140

on my first visit to the house, but before I could confirm it, Butch glanced at the painting and said, "It's the real thing, all right."

Jenna said, "Now how could you possibly know that? You barely glanced at it."

"Would you really like to know?" Butch said, barely able to hide his grin.

"Forget I asked," she said as David rejoined us.

"That was quick," I said.

"She's going to meet us at the shop," David said. After expressing her relief, Hannah undoubtedly had blistered him for taking off the way he had. I wasn't looking forward to being privy to part two of their little chat, but Fire at Will wasn't anywhere near the size of Tamra's house, and if they raised their voices above whispers, we'd all be able to hear what they were saying.

After David put Tamra's gun away properly and set the house alarm, Butch locked up and returned the key to its resting place. We then rode down the hill in relative silence. I half expected to see Sheriff Hodges waiting for us when we got back into town, but there was no sign of anyone in front of Fire at Will as Butch pulled into a parking space near my doorway. I normally liked to keep those spots open for new customers, but I wasn't about to ask Butch to move, not after all his help this morning.

He must have caught my glimpse, because as we were getting out, he stayed put. "I'm going to move this to the upper lot. I'll be right back."

"You don't have to," I said.

"But you wouldn't mind, would you?"

I was still looking for a polite way to answer when he grinned. "It's fine, Carolyn. I know the way you like to do business."

I unlocked the front door, and everyone went inside.

David looked around the shop, then asked, "So what do we do now?"

"There's not much we can do but wait," I said.

Sandy said, "I don't know about you guys, but I'm going to have a little fun while I'm here."

"That sounds delightful," Jenna said. "What shall we do?"

"Help yourselves," I said. "I've got some things I need to take care of. David can teach you anything you'd like to learn. Don't worry about fees; this lesson is on the house." I walked up front to work on my display a little more while they continued discussing which new project to try.

The front door chimed a few minutes

later, and I looked up, expecting to see Butch returning from parking his car, or even Hannah making an appearance.

What I had not expected to see was our illustrious sheriff.

At least not so soon.

"Where is he?" the sheriff demanded as he walked in.

"Who exactly are you looking for?" I asked. Not that I really had to guess, but he was using a tone of voice in my shop that I didn't approve of, at least not when it was directed at me.

"Don't get cute, Carolyn. I'm not in the mood for it."

"I wouldn't dream of it."

David poked his head around the corner. "Are you looking for me?"

"Where have you been?" the sheriff said as he moved toward him quickly. "Let's go. You're coming with me."

"Hold on, Sheriff," Jenna said as she joined us. "David has a right to an attorney, and I'm going to represent him, if he agrees to it."

"Sure, that would be great," David said.

Sheriff Hodges didn't look happy about the prospect, but there wasn't much he could do about it. "Are you really going to hide behind her?"

David started to reply, but Jenna touched his arm. "David, from now on, you're not to speak without express permission from me. Do you understand?"

Instead of answering, he just looked at her and nodded.

"Let's go," Sheriff Hodges snapped.

When I started to follow them out of the shop, he said, "Not you. You have no standing in this."

I looked at Jenna, who shook her head slightly.

Taking her cue, I said, "Fine, I'll stay here."

Jenna said, "Don't worry, I won't leave his side, and I'll call you the second I learn anything."

Butch came back in after they were gone. He found Sandy and me discussing what had just happened. "I leave you alone for five minutes, and now half the group's gone. Where's Jenna?"

"She's with David. The sheriff came by to talk to him, and Jenna agreed to represent him."

Butch smiled, and I added, "This is not the slightest bit funny."

"I'm just thinking about how Jenna's gonna shred him. Come on, don't you find that a little amusing?"

Sandy smiled. "I don't envy our sheriff. If we're not going to work on anything else, I'm going to go."

"Back to work?" I asked.

"Are you kidding? I'm taking a sick day, remember? No, I'm going to snoop around and see what I can find out about Richard Atkins."

Butch asked, "Would you like some company?"

"Sure, why not?" She looked at me and added, "Carolyn, you're more than welcome to come, too."

I was tempted, but I finally said, "No, I'd better stay here. I might get a customer. Stranger things have happened. Besides, Jenna expects me to be here, so I'm going to stay."

A little arm-twisting and I would have gone with them, but they both left, and I was at Fire at Will alone.

Not for long, though.

"Where is he?" Hannah asked as she stormed into the shop. "Where's David?"

"He's not here, Hannah." Before she could explode, I added, "The sheriff took him in for questioning, but don't worry, Jenna Blake's with him."

"And you just stood there and let it happen?"

"Well, I thought about stopping them, but the sheriff had a gun, and all I had was some pottery."

"Don't be ridiculous," she said.

"Then give me a little credit, will you? David's in good hands."

"I can do better than a retired judge," she snapped.

"In Maple Ridge? I doubt it. Let Jenna handle it, Hannah. She knows what she's doing. I'd let her defend my own sons, if it came to that."

"Good for you. I'm going to find someone else."

Before I could talk her out of it, Hannah was gone. Wow, a great many people were walking out on me today. The phone rang, and as I picked it up, I asked, "Jenna?"

"No, it's Bill. Your husband, remember?"

"Oh."

He paused a second, then said, "I've had warmer welcomes in my life. What's wrong?"

"What makes you sure something is? You don't know everything about me."

He chuckled, a sound I normally enjoyed. Just not at the moment. "What's so amusing?"

"I know enough. Now quit stalling and tell me what happened."

"If you must know, the sheriff came into the shop and took David in with him."

"When did he finally turn up?"

"The sheriff? About ten minutes ago. Why?"

"Not the sheriff, David. Stay focused, woman."

"David came to the shop this morning."

Bill hesitated, then asked, "Are you trying to tell me he just waltzed right in there of his own free will? Why don't I believe that you didn't have a hand in it?"

"You're just not very trusting, I guess," I said.

"With reason, from the sound of it. Does Hannah know where the boy is?"

"She left here thirty seconds ago. From the way she was talking, I expect to see Clarence Darrow's heir-apparent show up at any minute. She was pretty fired up when she left."

"Wouldn't you be? I don't suppose there's a chance in the world you're going to stay out of this, is there?"

"What do you think?"

"I know, I know, that's why I said that. Just be careful, okay? There's a killer loose in town."

"Why on earth would he come after me?" I asked, honestly startled by the premise.

"We don't know why he got Richard, do we? You could be next on his list."

"Or you," I retorted.

"Me? Why would anybody want to do me in? You're the closest thing to a threat on my life."

"Bill Emerson, why would you say something like that?" Sometimes my husband could utter the most inane things.

He laughed. "Cause you're the beneficiary on my life insurance policy."

"What is it, fifteen grand? You're worth more than that to me alive. Barely, but still."

"Hey, as long as it's in the plus column, I should be okay. If you need me, call. I'll be in my shop at the house, though, so leave a message and I'll get back to you as soon as I can."

"I'll be fine," I said, then I hung up the telephone. I'd grown accustomed to my husband's disappearances into his workshop. He was almost impossible to reach there, with all the constant sawing and hammering going on. I'd be in dire shape if I were depending on Bill coming to my rescue, especially if I had to get him on the telephone. My cell phone was charged enough, so I put it in my purse in case I'd need it later.

It was nearly lunch when Hannah came back to Fire at Will. She had two bags from Shelly's Café with her. "Feel like a quick bite with me?" she asked.

"That depends. Are you going to take my head off again?"

She looked contrite. "Carolyn, I'm sorry. When it comes to David, I tend to be a little overprotective sometimes."

"Really? I hadn't noticed. I'm surprised you're not with him right now. Is he still with the sheriff?"

"With the way Jenna was watching out for him? Hardly. She's quite vigorous defending him."

"So you're not getting a hired gun from New York or Los Angeles?"

"What gave you that idea?"

"When you left here, you said you were going for a legal-eagle gunslinger."

Hannah smiled. "I got one, too, didn't I?"

"David hired Jenna, remember?"

She snorted. "Does it really matter who chose her? They're back at Jenna's house now, deciding how to handle this. I was asked to leave, since the attorney-client privilege doesn't extend to mothers. Now are you going to accept my apology and eat with me, or do I have to have both burgers myself?"

"I forgive you," I said as I reached for one of the bags.

"You're too easy," she said, smiling.

"Hey, what can I say, you've found the best grease there is."

"Don't you like Shelly's burgers?"

I nodded. "Of course I do. I'm not talking about that kind of grease. I mean to make an apology go smoothly. Relationship lubrication is what I'm referring to."

"What can I say? I do my best," she said.

As we ate, we tried not to talk about what had happened to Richard, or why the police were focusing on David. It made for a strained conversation, but by the time we were finished eating, we were both at ease with each other again. I hated when Hannah and I fought, and I always felt better when we'd patched things up.

After we cleaned up, Hannah said, "I hate to eat and run, but I've got a class to teach."

"I thought you had TAs for that," I said.

"Believe it or not, some of us in the profession actually like to teach. Besides, my dear assistant is in love again, and that means her focus won't be on the modern novel."

"So, you feel pretty comfortable about Jenna helping David?"

"For the moment," she said. "I don't have much choice, do I? David insists that Jenna is the only lawyer he trusts, and if I'm hard-pressed, I'd probably have to agree. There's nothing I can do now, so I might as well teach my class."

I shrugged, and she must have read more into it than I'd meant to convey. "Do you think it's heartless, me teaching the day after my ex-husband died? I know women who would still be partying."

I looked her dead in the eyes. "But you're not that kind of woman, are you?"

"No, I'm not. I was devastated when Richard walked out on me, but that was a long time ago. Being with him wasn't all bad. We had our share of joy, and I got David in the bargain. Don't get me wrong, I wasn't about to nominate him for sainthood, but I didn't hate him. Now if I could just get the sheriff to believe me."

"Has he been pressuring you as well?"

"Let's just say he's keeping an eye on me. What are you doing about the situation?"

I picked up a glazed mug and pretended to study it. "What do you mean?"

"Carolyn Emerson, there's no way on earth you're standing idly by. I know you too well. You're looking into Richard's murder, aren't you?"

"I might have asked a few questions around town," I admitted reluctantly. The sheriff had already scolded me about my behavior, and my husband had as well. I wasn't in the mood to hear it from Hannah, too.

She shocked me by saying, "Well, keep it up. Don't let anyone talk you out of it."

"Excuse me for saying so, but you're usually not this supportive when I start snooping." That was an understatement.

"I've got a vested interest this time. Besides, if the sheriff is focusing on David and me, somebody else has to look for the real killer. Keep me posted, okay?"

"Sure," I promised.

After Hannah had gone, I wondered about her change of heart. Did she want to be notified of my progress for David's sake, or for her own? I might have to wonder about that, if I were a suspicious person, which normally I wasn't. Well, I wasn't. Okay, maybe sometimes, but only if it was merited. Anyway, it could be argued that Hannah wanted to know what I was up to so she could see if I was getting too close to the truth. Could she have had something to do with Richard's murder, despite her earlier declaration? Or did she believe in her heart that David had killed his own father in some kind of fit of rage? Nonsense, I couldn't believe it of my best friend in the world, or her son. Still, just to be cautious, I decided it couldn't hurt to keep quiet about what I found out, at least until I was able to come up with something definitive.

"Hi, is this where I can paint my own pottery?" a petite young woman with fine blonde hair asked as she came into the shop an hour before closing.

"This is the place," I said, trying to keep my sarcasm to myself. I looked around at the bisqueware, the bottles of paint and glaze, and the tables, and wondered what else she thought it might be. "Is there anything in particular you're interested in?"

"I think I'll look around first," she said.

"Be my guest. If there's anything you need, just let me know." I wasn't exactly worried about shoplifting, at least not from the unglazed section; some of the pieces I had on display were worth quite a bit of money, but I figured it'd be difficult for her to get a teapot under her dress, as snugly as it fit.

It was fascinating watching her study each item in turn, picking it up, looking at all sides of it, then placing it delicately back down. Forty-five minutes later, she was still just halfway through my stock. "I'm afraid if you don't make a selection soon, there won't be time to decorate it," I told her.

She looked pensively at me. "I just hate to rush my decision."

"I understand," which was a total and complete lie if there ever was one. "I just thought you should know."

"Perhaps I should come back tomorrow."

People took less time to choose a mate. "I'll be here."

She thought about that another minute. "That's what I'll do then. I'll come back tomorrow."

That's what she said. What she did was just stand there, staring at the pottery she'd yet to examine. Finally, reluctantly, she left. I couldn't wait for her return. If David managed to come into work the next day, she was all his. Maybe with my handsome young assistant she'd make a decision in less than a month.

I normally hated to close the place early, but that woman had gotten under my skin. So what if I lost a customer or two? I flipped the sign, dead-bolted the door, then started cashing out the register.

I'd just started my report when I heard a knock at the front door. "We're closed," I called out without looking up.

"Open up the door, you daft old woman," my husband, Bill, called out from the sidewalk.

I walked over to the door, but I didn't unlock it. "You'll need to talk a little sweeter than that if you expect me to comply."

He stared at me a few seconds, as if deciding what to do, then grinned slyly. "If you don't let me in, you won't know why I'm here. Let's see your curiosity stand that."

"I can take it if you can," I said, turning my back on him. Honestly, the man should have learned by now not to order me around. I gave it thirty seconds, then turned back to him.

He was gone.

But where? I leaned out through my display window trying to catch sight of him, but my field of vision was limited to a few squares of the sidewalk on each side of my shop. I unlocked the door, and the second I did, he popped out from next door.

"Got you," he said with delight.

"Get inside, you old goat."

"Now who needs to talk sweet?" he asked. "It's not nice, calling your husband an old goat."

"Which part do you object to, 'old' or 'goat'?"

He frowned. "Both of them. What do you think?"

"I think they fit, sometimes," I said. I noticed a few window-shoppers looking our way. "Now get inside. You're making a scene."

As he followed me into Fire at Will, he said, "You were the one yelling."

"I was not yelling," I said, trying to keep my voice soft. I had a tendency, when aggravated, to increase my volume, or so I've been told. I wasn't sure it was true, but enough people had pointed it out that I was beginning to doubt it could be a conspiracy. "Now what is your news?"

"Speak up. I can barely hear you," Bill said, cocking one hand behind an ear.

"You heard me just fine, and you know it. What's going on?"

"I got another commission," he said. "It's for five Shaker-style nightstands for a bed-and-breakfast over in Newberry."

"Olive Haslett is working you too hard." Olive owned the business Shaker Styles where my husband was employed. What had started out as a hobby after his retirement had developed into a full-time job.

"Olive's got nothing to do with this," he said. "I got this order on my own."

"Do you mean to tell me you're soliciting

156

business on the side? Don't you have enough to do?"

He said, "I thought you'd be happier about it. I'll make twice as much as I do working for Olive."

"We don't need the money," I said. "Besides, you're supposed to be retired and enjoying yourself."

"If I had to sit on that rocking chair on the porch all day waiting for you to come home, I'd climb up on the roof just so I could throw myself off."

"Gee, thanks. I was wrong before. You know just what to say to get my heart fluttering."

He took me in his arms, something that still managed to take my breath away after all the years. "You know what I mean."

"I do," I said. "You need to stay busy to be happy."

He pulled away and smiled. "That's what I just said."

"In what language, Urdu? That might be what you meant, but it was certainly not what you said."

"Don't quibble," he said as he reached into his pocket and pulled out a card. "What do you think?"

I looked at it and saw an old-fashioned wooden hand-plane on it, along with my husb d's name and telephone number. Above it all, in bold letters, it said, "Old-Fashioned." I handed it back to him. "Is that the best name you could come up with for your business?"

He took the card back, studied it a second, then frowned. "What's wrong with it?"

"Since I know for a fact that you're not a bartender or a spinster, I'm not sure what you're trying to say."

"It's furniture, and you know it."

I tapped the card. "I know it because I know you, but someone else might not. Why don't you add the word 'furniture' below it, if you're stuck on the first part."

"I could write it in with a pen," he said as he looked at the card yet again.

"You will do no such thing. Your handwriting's a mess."

"You could do it, then," he said.

"I could, but I'm not going to. Let me think about it a minute." I started playing with names, trying to come up with something more clever than "Old-Fashioned." It certainly shouldn't be that hard. "How about 'Brand New Antiques'?"

He thought about it, then said, "Yeah, that's kind of nice. I'll have new cards made up when I run out of these."

"How many did you have made up?"

158

"I got a deal on a thousand. That's not bad for twenty bucks, is it?"

I reached over into the till and pulled out a twenty. "I'll trade you this bill for the rest of your cards. That way you'll break even."

"You should make it forty for me to do that," he said.

"If that's the way you're going to be, give me back my twenty and you can pay for the new ones as well."

"Not so fast. I was just kidding," he said. "You free for dinner? I feel like celebrating."

"That sounds wonderful," I said, dreaming of a night out on the town. "What did you have in mind?"

He scratched his chin, then said, "You haven't made meatloaf in a while."

"Thanks, but I'll pass."

"How about fried chicken? You make the best in town."

I stood toe-to-toe with my husband. "Bill Emerson, my idea of celebrating isn't cooking for you at home. You should take me out to dinner."

He nodded. "Sorry, I guess you're right. There's just nothing in the world I'd rather have than your meatloaf."

How sweet. I knew when he was conning me and when he wasn't, and the expression on his face told me that my husband was sincere. "Tell you what. Why don't we go out some other time. All of sudden, meatloaf sounds great to me, too."

"I didn't think you wanted to make it."

"Are you going to argue with me, or are you going to take a list and pick up a few things at the store for me?" We had a routine when I was cooking a meal he'd requested: I'd do the work, but he had to shop. I knew how much he disliked the grocery store, and if my dear husband was willing to do that, then I knew he was serious.

"Just tell me what you need," he said.

I jotted down the ingredients, along with potatoes and some frozen peas. He took it from me and studied it. "There's no pie on here."

"You didn't ask for pie," I said. "I don't have time to make a crust."

"We could get a lemon meringue from the store," he said.

I knew it was his favorite dessert. "Go ahead, pick one up, too. You're going to get fat if you keep eating those things. You know that, don't you?"

"Are you kidding? For pie, I'm willing to take the risk. Any chance you want to come with me to the grocery?"

I could have managed it, but I still wanted

to check in with the Firing Squad members before I left the shop. "I'll be along in half an hour. Now shoo."

He started for the door, then said, "Thanks."

"For what?"

"Understanding your crazy old husband," he said with a grin.

"I don't know that I'll ever understand you," I said, returning his smile, "but after nearly thirty years of being married to you, I've learned to just accept you the way you are."

"Then it's been time well spent," he said, a surprisingly gushy remark coming from my normally gruff husband.

"I think so," I admitted. I locked up behind him, and suddenly regretted not going with him to the store. After all, he was being such a dear. On a whim, I shoved the cash from the till into the pig, turned off the lights, and locked the shop up. The investigation could wait.

For now, I wanted to be with my husband.

"I'm sorry to call you at home, but this is kind of important," Butch said after I picked up the phone later that night. Bill and I had enjoyed the meatloaf, and I'd even joined him in a piece of pie. I'd walk to the shop

161

tomorrow to make up for it, I promised myself.

"It's okay," I said. "What's going on?"

"I've been talking with Sandy, and we'd like to get together tonight, if it's not too much trouble."

"I'm surprised you didn't wrangle Jenna in, too," I said.

"That's part of what we need to talk to you about," Butch replied. "Can you come down to Fire at Will?"

How could I say no, especially since I was the one who'd gotten them involved in the first place? "Give me ten minutes," I said.

"That's fine. We'll be there."

I grabbed my purse and my jacket, then nudged Bill, who had fallen asleep in front of the television, the Discovery Channel blaring out. "I'm going out for a while," I said.

"You want me to come with you?" he asked groggily.

"No, I'd hate to interrupt your program."

He glanced at the television. "What happened to *MythBusters*? Did you change the channel?"

"They went off twenty minutes ago," I said. "You fell asleep."

"I was just resting my eyes," he said.

"Then you should have given your snoring a rest, too," I said. "I won't be long."

He nodded. "Do I even need to ask what this is about?"

"You can ask, but I'm fairly certain you won't like my answer, so maybe we should just leave it at that."

"Maybe we should," he said. "Be careful."

I leaned over and kissed his forehead. "I promise."

"I'll be here when you get back."

"I'd expect nothing less," I said.

I could have walked to the shop and atoned for my slice of pie, but it was dark out, and the wind had picked up enough to put a chill in the air.

The exercise would have to wait. Butch had sounded urgent, and I needed to get to the shop and learn what my crew had found out.

Chapter 8

"Thanks for coming," Butch said as I walked up to the pottery shop. "I hate to drag you out like this."

"Where are the others?" I asked as I fumbled with my keys. "Or did you already let them in?" Butch was a reformed burglar, so I knew my feeble security system was no match for his skills. Sometimes I wondered just how "former" he really was, but I was too afraid he'd tell me the truth if I asked him.

"I'd never do that," he said. "At least not without your permission. Sandy will be here any second. In fact, here she comes right now."

Sandy approached us with a tray of coffees and a bag from In the Grounds. "I've got treats," she said.

"You didn't have to do that," I protested. "We could have made coffee inside," I added as I opened the door.

"This way's quicker," she said.

After I locked the door behind us and flipped on a few lights, I asked, "So, why isn't Jenna coming tonight?"

"That's the thing," Butch said. "When I called her and asked her to come, she said she couldn't."

"That's perfectly understandable," I said as I sipped some of the warm coffee. "We all can't drop our lives at a moment's notice and come running."

"You don't understand. She didn't bail on us because she was busy. Now that she's representing David, Jenna didn't feel that it was right for her to help us with our snooping."

"It's all for the same cause, Butch," Sandy said. "I still think you're overreacting."

"Sometimes she gets a little carried away with those ethics of hers," Butch said.

"We have to respect her position," I said. "Until Martha gets back, the three of us will have to just muddle along. Was that it, then? We could have had this conversation over the phone."

Butch shook his head. "No, we're just getting started. Sandy and I have found out a lot of important information today."

"That doesn't surprise me at all," I said.

"Let's hear it. We're all here, and I'm listening."

"You go first," Butch told Sandy.

"Okay. I went back to the library after hours and tapped into some records for the county."

I wasn't sure I liked the sound of that, even if it was for a good cause. "Is that legal? I don't want you getting into trouble on David's account. One member of the Firing Squad in the sheriff's sights is enough."

"Don't worry, it's all a matter of public record. The thing is, you have to know where to look. They do their best to obfuscate the information, but I'm on to their tricks. It turns out our fair mayor isn't quite the success he wants everyone to believe. Harvey Jenkins is not really the sole proprietor of his business at all. He barely has a quarter share of ownership."

"Sandy, forgive me, but what does this have to do with Richard Atkins?"

"I'm getting to that. It turns out that the majority owner is a company called Clay-Date."

"I'm sorry, perhaps I'm slow because it's getting so late. What's the significance to our investigation?"

"ClayDate is a dummy corporation, and I saw a reference to an R. A. Potter in the incorporation papers. It has to be Richard Atkins. Don't you see? Richard Atkins, Potter."

"It doesn't have to be," I said, a little impatiently. "It could be Regina Ann, Reginald Allen, or Rebecca Alison."

Sandy frowned. "I have a hard time believing that. I would have dug a little deeper, but I wanted to get back here to tell you. I actually thought I'd found something."

"You may have," I said. "We just need to investigate a little more. It's true that Richard and Harvey were in business together a long time ago, but from everything I've heard, it ended when Richard left Hannah twenty years ago."

I turned to Butch. "How about you? What did you find out? I don't suppose you were digging around on the Internet as well, were you?"

"Hardly. I like a more direct approach when I snoop around. I was talking to an old friend of mine, and he had an interesting light to shed on this mess. I know he's your uncle, but Don Rutledge is not a good guy."

"Do you think that's news to me?"

"No, but this might be. From what I heard tonight, he was out at the college asking questions about Charles Potter. He doesn't strike me as the crafting type, but I could be wrong."

"You're not," I said. "My uncle is many things, but that's not one of them. So, you think he knew that Charles Potter and Richard Atkins were one and the same before the rest of us?"

"He had to."

"I'm not as certain as you are, but I have to admit, it doesn't look like he's completely innocent in all of this, does it?"

Butch shrugged. "I don't care so much about guilt and innocence. I'm more concerned with results. We find out who aced the potter and David walks. It's as simple as that."

"It doesn't sound all that straightforward to me," I said. "Anything else?"

Butch scratched his chin. "There's Rose to dig into, and Kendra Williams, too."

"What a joy. If you're right about either one of them, I'm working on murderer's row."

"As long as you're not next in line," Butch said.

"I'll second that," said Sandy. She glanced at my Dali-inspired clock. "Is that the time? I've got to go."

"Late for a big date?" I asked.

"I wish. No, I've got a meeting first thing

in the morning. Corki's got a big announcement to make, and she asked me to come in early."

"What's she up to?"

"With her, she's probably going to take a sabbatical and climb Denali."

"The bottled water?" Butch asked.

"No, the mountain in Alaska, and stop pretending you didn't know that. Good night."

"Let me walk you to your car," Butch said.

"I'm perfectly capable of making it on my own," Sandy said.

"I know. I was kind of hoping you could protect me in case there are any bad guys out and about tonight," he said with a grin.

"Come on, you big lug," she said. "Carolyn, are you coming with us?"

I thought about catching up on my account books since I was already there, but it was late, I was tired, and I had no desire to walk to my car alone later.

"I'm right behind you."

"It's a lot more fun if we're side by side," Sandy said.

"Just go," I replied.

When I walked back into the house, Bill was still awake and the television was off. I took my jacket off and asked, "What happened? I thought your next program was on."

"I couldn't enjoy it knowing you were out there by yourself."

"Don't give me that nonsense," I said as I hung my coat up. "You know I can take care of myself."

"I can still worry about you, can't I?"

"I suppose," I said as I leaned forward and kissed his forehead. As I did so, I brushed the remote control with my knee, and the television jumped to life. It was tuned to his usual channel, but the program wasn't the one he normally watched. "Preempted, was it?"

He shrugged. "I still would have watched it. You know me."

"I do at that. Coming to bed?"

"I'll be up in a bit. This looks kind of interesting."

I left him to his show and decided to take a quick shower before bed. As I scrubbed up, I thought about what Sandy and Butch had said. Was there any possibility that the R. A. Potter she'd found referenced to was actually Hannah's ex-husband? That would mean that he'd kept in a lot closer contact with Maple Ridge than anyone had realized. Then again, it was probably Ramona and not Richard, just one big coincidence.

Butch's news, on the other hand, might have more substance to it. Don had a reason to want to see Richard suffer, and knowing how long my uncle could hold a grudge, I wouldn't put anything past him. I knew he believed in his heart that the reason he was alone was because of Richard Atkins. I didn't buy his story that he and Rose were just friends. I wondered if Rose felt the same way about Dan. It would certainly give either one of them a motive for murder if they believed that Richard had robbed them of their one chance for happiness.

And what about Kendra Williams and Harvey Jenkins?

Could I imagine Kendra killing the man? Or Rose, for that matter? I'd never been all that fond of car salesmen, including the mayor. I could easily believe that Harvey Jenkins had killed Richard, but wishing didn't make it so.

David and Hannah were decidedly not on my list of suspects. And if I was being honest about it, I wouldn't have added their names to the list even if I'd seen either one of them do it myself.

I was just falling asleep when something occurred to me. If Richard had been keeping tabs on Maple Ridge from afar, what would have made him come back, thereby blowing his cover identity as Charles Potter? Had he returned to get to know David, as he'd told me before he died, or did he have a more sinister motivation? He'd managed to build a new life for himself, so why risk it all now?

I wasn't sure, but I was only getting more muddled trying to figure everything out when I was so tired. It was going to have to wait until tomorrow.

"You're up early," Bill said as he joined me at the breakfast table the next morning.

"I've got some errands to run before I open the shop," I said.

"Carolyn, you're not going to give up on this, are you? What's it going to take, someone whacking you in the middle of the night like they did Richard Atkins?"

"No, but thanks for that thought. What a perfect way to start the day." My husband had a way of pointing out my sometimes foolish behavior in ways that were a little more descriptive than I liked.

"You need to remember what could happen to you," he said. "You're not bulletproof."

"I'm careful, and you know it," I said. "Don't worry so much. I'll see you tonight."

"I surely hope so," he said as I left. What

a glum mood my husband was in. I couldn't help but take some of his bleak outlook to heart as I drove to Fire at Will. Was I wasting my time, trying to investigate a crime the police were already looking into? Knowing Sheriff Hodges as I did, I was skeptical about just how hard he would investigate. If he had David and Hannah already pegged as his only two suspects, it would certainly take more evidence than what I'd uncovered so far to dissuade him of the idea. I needed proof. The only problem was, I wasn't exactly sure how to go about getting any.

Breaking my own rule, I decided to keep the Intrigue close, so I parked on the street four storefronts down from my shop. I wanted to be able to go when I needed to, not slog halfway through town before I could get to my car.

I glanced in the window of Fire at Will, but I kept walking. Everything looked normal enough inside, and I had plenty of work to do, but my errand had to take precedence. I knew Kendra was usually at her shop, Hattie's Attic, by seven every morning, doing what, I had no idea. It was nearly eight, but the shop was dark and the sign still said she was closed. Where could she be? Was she sleeping in, or was it something more ominous? Stop it, I chided myself. You've jumped to enough conclusions this week, thank you very much. If Kendra isn't here, she must have a good reason.

Rose was already at Rose Colored Glasses, though I knew that she never opened before ten.

I tested the door, and sure enough, it was unlocked. As I walked in, Rose said, "Sorry, we're not really open yet."

"It's me," I said.

She looked up, obviously startled by my sudden appearance. "Carolyn, what are you doing here?"

"I'm fine, Rose. How are you?" She was trying to be rude, in her own way, but I wasn't going to let her get away with it. The sarcasm in my voice had to be evident.

"I didn't mean to snap at you. Sorry," she said again, her face reddened. It was the curse of her complexion. Rose Nygren couldn't hide her discomfort from me, or anyone else.

"I'd like to talk more about Richard Atkins. We didn't get a chance to finish last time we spoke."

"I don't want to discuss him, Carolyn. That's all ancient history. I've moved on."

I looked around the shop. "Have you? Rose, have you even dated anyone since

Richard left town?"

"I've had an active enough social life," she said. "Not that it's any of your business." The woman looked ready to bolt from her own store, but I stood my ground.

"When he was murdered in my backyard, it became my business," I said. "I've spoken with my uncle," I added softly.

"How is he?" she asked, all the anger suddenly gone from her voice. "I regret what happened between Don and me more than anything about the whole affair." She paused, then amended, "Okay, that was a bad choice of words. 'Incident' doesn't sound much better. Let's just leave it at that."

"My uncle's as mean as ever. I can't imagine you two were ever friends, let alone anything more." I was baiting her, I couldn't deny it, but I meant what I said. Even though we were blood kin, I could barely stand to be around Don Rutledge. Why should Rose feel any differently?

"He wasn't always like he is now," she said.

"He has been as long as I can remember, and that's at least forty-five years."

Rose blushed again, slightly this time, then said, "I should have said he wasn't like that with me."

"You had a crush on him, didn't you?" The words just popped out of my mouth, but that didn't mean I didn't believe them. There was no denying the look in her eyes when she spoke about my uncle.

"We were friends," she repeated.

"But you wanted it to be more, didn't you? You lost something dear to you when Don found out about you and Richard. Where were you the night before last, Rose?"

"Carolyn, are you asking me for an alibi?" She was ready to snap, and for once, I was happy to supply the extra nudge she needed. If I could get her to break down, maybe I could get the truth out of her.

"I'll do one better than that. I'm asking you if you killed Richard Atkins."

I had hoped I'd pushed her enough to get a response, but not the one she gave me. Rose Nygren's eyes rolled into the back of her head, and she fainted dead away.

I grabbed some water from her bathroom and splashed a little on her face. "Rose? Are you all right?" I thought about calling 911, but I wasn't sure if I should. I'd try to wake her on my own, and if that failed, then I'd call for the paramedics.

Her eyelids fluttered, and then opened. "Carolyn? What happened?"

"You fainted," I said. "Are you feeling any better?"

The memory of how I'd accused her must have swept across her because she said quickly, "You need to leave."

"I'm not going to go and leave you lying on the floor," I protested.

She struggled to stand, then leaned against a shelf and pulled herself up. "I'm fine. Now go."

"You should see somebody, a doctor," I said.

"I skipped breakfast, so I was a little light-headed. I mean it. You aren't welcome here."

"Fine, but I'm going to check in on you later." She couldn't keep me from doing that, could she?

"If you do, I'm calling Sheriff Hodges and telling him that you've been harassing me. That's what you're doing, you know."

"I'm just trying to find out what happened to Richard Atkins," I said.

"Leave me alone." Her voice was shrill, and I didn't want her to faint again, so I did as she asked and left. How curious her behavior had been. I wasn't quite sure what to make of it. I didn't have much time to dally, though. If I was going to speak with Harvey Jenkins before it was time to open my shop, I'd have to hurry. I rushed back to the Intrigue and headed for his car lot.

Harvey was out front, changing the cardboard sign he had in the window of a Subaru. That wasn't his only manufacturer; since Maple Ridge was a small town, Harvey carried a variety of new vehicles.

"Have you finally come in to trade that Intrigue?" he asked the second he saw me. "I can make you a sweet deal on a new Subaru. We've got a new shipment of Honda CRVs, too."

"Thanks, but I'm just here to talk to you."

"Unless it's about a new car, I don't have the time. This is a busy season for me."

I looked around the deserted parking lot. "I can see you're just swamped with customers."

"You never know, a crowd could be five minutes away."

From the intent jut of his jaw, I realized he was serious. "Fine. I'll test drive that one."

"Sounds good. Let me get a plate and we'll be off."

I looked at the red vehicle, and found that I liked its sporty style. My Intrigue was great, and I loved it, but that didn't mean it was the last car I ever wanted to own. Besides, if we were riding together Harvey would be a captive audience.

Harvey attached the plate and handed me the keys. "You're going to love this. It's really got some pep."

I took the keys, got in, and started it up. We were twenty feet out of the parking lot when Harvey started to press. "Now let's talk about this ride. It's got four-wheel independent suspension, a 173-horsepower engine, and sixteen-inch alloy wheels."

"Stop," I said. "The more you talk, the less I like it."

He shut up as if I'd thrown a switch. We drove a few miles — and I had to admit, I liked the way it handled — then I decided to get to why I was really there.

"I'm sorry about your loss," I said.

"What are you talking about?" Harvey answered.

"Your partner died a few nights ago. That's got to be tough on you."

"I don't have a partner," he said.

"You might be able to fool the rest of the world, but I know Richard Atkins owned a percentage of your business through Clay-Date."

I'd expected a denial, not the laughter I got instead. "That's a blast from the past. That particular business has been dead twenty years. You should do your homework, Carolyn. It's old news."

Could Sandy, in her haste, have found dated information? I had to press it, regardless. Now that Harvey knew what I was up to, I'd given away the advantage of surprise. "Are you trying to tell me you didn't lose a fortune when Richard skipped out of town?"

"I'd hardly call what I lost a fortune. I'd honestly forgotten all about the man until this week. I've had my share of good partners and bad ones, but I don't hold grudges, and I don't look back. Now, what do you think?"

"About what?"

"The car. She's a real beauty, isn't she?"

I'd honestly forgotten the ruse. "It's a machine, not a female. Why must men do that?"

"Not all men, not all the time," he said. "You've got to admit, this car handles better than yours."

"I don't have to admit anything," I said. "I love my Intrigue."

He grinned. "What happened to vehicles just being machines?"

"Are you trying to lose a sale?" I said. I turned the car around and headed back to his lot.

"Hey, I was just kidding."

"Sorry, I've changed my mind." I didn't want a new vehicle, couldn't afford the pay-

180

ments if I did, and wouldn't buy it from Harvey Jenkins even if the first two points didn't matter.

Back at the dealership, I pulled to a stop, turned off the engine, but kept the keys in my hand.

He reached for them, but I held back. "There's one more thing I want to ask you."

"Go ahead," he said warily.

"Where were you two nights ago?"

Harvey shook his head. "That's none of your business."

"What happened to treating the customer right?"

"You don't have any intention of buying a new car," he said. "Now give me the keys."

I thought about holding on to them, but changed my mind and dropped them in his extended palm. As I got out, I said, "Thanks for the test drive."

"Sure thing," he said, barely managing to suppress a snarl. It was gone as quickly as it had come, and as he turned to greet a new customer, I could see his usual smarmy smile plastered to his face. "Hi there, I see you're admiring the new model. She's a beauty, isn't she?"

I got back into the Intrigue and headed to Fire at Will. I wasn't sure I'd accomplished anything that morning other than alienating more people, but I couldn't worry about that. I had a murder to solve and a business to run, in that order.

Someone was waiting for me to open, and for a second, I didn't recognize him. As I neared the shop, though, I saw that it was my cottage-making customer. That was stretching things, as I'd done all the work, but it was nice to see someone interested in my shop, for whatever the reason.

"I know it's early," he said the second I pulled out my key. "I just couldn't wait."

"Impatient to see how it turned out?" I asked as I unlocked the door.

"No, that's not it, though I am rather curious. It's for my mother, and I'm afraid she won't make it until noon."

It stunned me the man's mother could even still be alive, given the years he must have logged himself. "I'm so sorry," I said as I led him in. I didn't care that I wasn't set to open for another ten minutes. He might not have that long.

"Don't be," he said. "She's had a good life, made a great many friends, and helped scores of people over the years. Her last wish was to see her cottage in Haymore one last time, and since the sweet old thing would never last the trip, I commissioned you to make one for me. All the old photographs were lost in a fire, and I'm hoping my memory is strong enough to match Mother's."

It was the sweetest thing I'd ever heard. "It should be ready. Let's go check."

I opened the kiln, holding my breath as I peered inside. We lose things sometimes when we fire them. It's the nature of the business, and not a pleasant part of it, at that. I just hoped and prayed that the cottage we'd created made it.

I reached in and pulled it out. The glazes and paints had turned out beautifully, and I could see why my customer's mother would long for it in her last days. I wouldn't mind living there myself.

I handed it to him, which he took reverently. "It's perfect," he said, his voice muted.

"It did turn out rather well." I retrieved my effort, and was pleased with it, too.

"That's very nice, too," he said. "Pardon me for asking, but is it for sale?"

I smiled at him. "If it's not bolted down, it's for sale. And don't worry about offending me. I'd be delighted to sell it to you."

He nodded his approval. "Wrap them both then, would you, please?"

"I'll take care of it." We hadn't yet discussed a price, and honestly, what he'd paid to have the firings expedited would cover the bill for both of them. I wasn't sure he'd stand for that though; I decided I'd give him a great price on the pair of cottages.

I came back up front and handed him the two cottages, each wrapped carefully and boxed. "Here you go."

He took them from me and handed me an envelope. "And here you are."

"Thanks. But we didn't discuss a price."

"I think you'll find that suitable," he said, and then he was gone.

I opened up the envelope, not sure what I would find, and was startled to see only a letter inside. It was a flyer for an antique auction in Bloodsbury.

I couldn't believe he'd stiffed me. He'd seemed like such a nice man. It wasn't that I'd lose any money on the transaction given his earlier firing fee, but it was a rather petty way of getting out of paying the final bill.

I took out a pin and tacked the flyer to the board behind the register where I kept the delinquent checks I got from time to time. It would serve as a reminder that I was running a business, not a charity shop. It served me right. I'd neglected to name a price, so he'd neglected to pay it.

I did hate losing that cottage for nothing, though. I decided to make another one and put it in the display window. Something good might come of this after all.

I was just putting the walls of my latest effort together when David walked in.

"I wasn't sure I'd be seeing you today," I said.

"Sorry I'm late. I had some problems I had to deal with." He looked absolutely hangdog.

"Is the sheriff giving you trouble?" Had Hodges amped up his pursuit of David as the killer?

"I almost wish it had been that. You know what? I don't think I'm one of his major suspects anymore."

"What makes you say that?"

David shrugged. "He wants an easy arrest, but I think he knows I'm not guilty."

"Then why are you so glum?"

He looked as if he wanted to cry as he said, "Annie broke up with me."

"How awful for you," I said. "Did she say why?"

"Oh yes, in complete and thorough detail. It appears that I've been less than the ideal boyfriend, and she kindly pointed out several ways I could improve myself in the future, were I ever lucky enough to make the acquaintance of a girl of her caliber again."

"Ouch, that had to sting," I said as I

added the roof. It surprised me when I realized that I was making a cottage just like the one I'd done for my customer. I wasn't sure why, but something about the place seemed to beckon to me.

"You don't seem all that sympathetic," David said a little truculently.

"For sympathy, you should go to your mother. For the truth, I'll do just as well as anyone else will."

David's face dropped. "So, you think she's right?"

"David, my dear, sweet friend, how should I know? Only two people ever really know what goes wrong with a relationship, but it sounds as though Annie gave you some things to think about. Take her advice, and maybe you'll do better next time."

"I wanted to do better this time," he admitted.

"Sorry, I can't help you there, either. Annie's a fine young woman, but I'm sure she's not the only eligible one in Maple Ridge."

"I guess," David said. Then, for the first time since walking in, he seemed to notice what I was doing. "Model building?"

"No, this is real construction. We should do more of these for our paint crowd," I said.

"They'd have to cost a fortune," David

said. "Making them looks pretty labor inten-
sive."

"All it costs us is time and clay, and we've
got plenty of each at the moment. Grab
some clay and start building."

"Sure, why not? What should I build?"

"Visualize your dream house," I said, "and
then make it happen."

"As easy as that?"

"It can be, if you want it to," I said.

By the time I'd finished my replica of the
cottage, David was lost in a design of his
own. He was right about his concerns of
how much to charge for them. A great deal
of time and effort went into each piece, but
I didn't care. By building cottages and
bisque-firing them for our customers, we
were offering them more choices than the
norm of cups, mugs, plates, and saucers.

David studied the house he was building,
then said softly, "You know, the worst part
of it is that she was right, all the way across
the board."

I patted his shoulder. "Just remember,
where there's life, there's hope. Nobody's
born knowing how to date. That's why you
do so much of it. Believe it or not, you get
better with practice."

"Then I'd better get started. Do you have
any candidates for me?"

"No thanks, I'm not about to set you up on any blind dates," I said, as the front door chimed.

I was ready to wait on a new customer when I saw it was my uncle Don.

"We need to talk. Right now," he said, the fire leaping from his glare.

CHAPTER 9

"Go ahead, I'm listening."

"Not here. Out there," Don said as he pointed to the sidewalk in front of Fire at Will.

David looked at me, and I shrugged. If my uncle didn't want to talk in front of my assistant, that was fine with me.

I followed him out, and I was barely onto the street when he snarled, "Don't you ever go after Rose Nygren again, do you hear me?"

"What are you talking about?"

"I understand you went by her store and was browbeating her," he snapped. "You have no right."

"How did you hear about it?" I asked.

"Rose called me," he admitted.

"I thought you two were estranged." This was getting interesting. I'd meant to stir things up in Maple Ridge with my inquiries, but I was beginning to realize that I might be stirring up more than I'd bargained for.

"We were, but she didn't know who else to call."

"I find that interesting, don't you?" I asked. I never would have believed it, but my uncle's voice actually softened whenever he talked about Rose. "After all, it's been a long time."

"Too long," he admitted, "but you're missing the point."

"Am I?"

"Don't be that way, Carolyn. It wasn't cute when you were a kid, and it's surely not attractive now. Leave her alone, or you'll wish you'd listened to me." He smacked one hand with the other, and the ring I'd noticed earlier caught the light. I'd hate to think what it would do if he hit me.

"Are you threatening me? What happened to blood being thicker than water?"

"Don't count too much on that," he said, then stormed off.

I looked around to see if anyone had witnessed the confrontation, and saw Kendra ducking back into her shop. She'd no doubt seen and heard everything.

I still needed to talk to her, and David was minding the store, so I pulled off my apron and hurried over to Hattie's Attic before Kendra could call half of Maple Ridge and tell them what she'd just seen.

She looked startled to see me enter her shop, and as I'd suspected, Kendra had her telephone firmly in her hand. "Carolyn, I wasn't expecting to see you."

"Put the phone down, Kendra. We need to talk."

She looked at me warily. "I'm busy right now."

"So am I," I said. "This won't take long."

There wasn't a soul in her shop besides the two of us, so at least I had that in my favor. "I want to talk to you about Richard Atkins."

"We've had this conversation, Carolyn. You're repeating yourself."

"Where were you two nights ago?"

Kendra just smiled. "Wouldn't you like to know."

"I'm not digging into your social life. I just want to be able to eliminate you as a suspect."

Kendra shook her head. "I'd love to help you, but I'm afraid I'm not at liberty to discuss that. There are other people's lives involved."

"Just give me a name, Kendra, and I'll get off your back. I promise."

"As I said, it's none of your business."

"Why does everyone keep saying that? It's a simple question."

The door chimed, and David hurried in. "Carolyn, I was hoping I'd find you here."

"What's going on?" The look on his face told me something was seriously wrong.

"You'd better get back to the shop. Something's happened."

Kendra butted in. "What is it? What's going on?"

"Sorry, I need to talk to Carolyn about it first."

I followed him out of Hattie's Attic, but I wasn't going to wait until we got back to the shop to find out what had brought him out searching for me so urgently.

I put a hand on his arm to stop him. "David, what is it?"

"It's Bill. There's been an accident."

I felt my heart stop. "What happened?"

"I don't know all the details. He was working in his shop and something happened."

I raced toward Fire at Will to get my car keys. "How bad is it?"

"Carolyn, all I know is that he's in the emergency room. Come on, you're in no shape to drive. I'll take you."

"I'm not riding on the back of your motorcycle," I said.

"We can take your car, but you don't need

to add to your problems right now. I hope you don't mind, but I already locked the shop up and I grabbed your keys."

"Of course I don't mind. Let's go." As we got into the car, I asked, "What exactly did the hospital say?"

"They didn't call," he admitted. "Annie was there visiting her aunt and she saw him come in. That's all I know."

I nodded, too numb to speak. What had happened? Had Bill had an accident with one of his woodworking machines? Had he had a heart attack? A thousand scenarios raced through my mind. I'd have to call the boys, but not until after I knew what had happened. They'd want to come back home to be with their father. I'd need to change the linens in the guest room and pull a cot out of the garage. Then there was food to worry about. Oh Lord, what was my mind doing? I was probably thinking about the arrangements because it was something I could actually control. What had happened to my dear, sweet, ornery husband?

David pulled up at the ER doors. "You go on. I'll park and then join you."

I shot out of the car without even thanking him. There were several people in the waiting room, but no sign of Bill. It must have been urgent if they'd taken him straight back. I approached the nurse's station. "I'm here to see my husband."

The nurse, buried in paperwork behind her desk, held up one finger. "Hang on a second."

"His name's Bill Emerson," I said.

"You're going to have to wait."

There wasn't much chance of that. Since she wasn't being helpful, I decided to find someone who was. I started back to the treatment area when the security guard on duty blocked my path. "I'm afraid you can't go in there, ma'am."

"If you think you're going to stop me, you'd better pull out that gun, because I'm going in."

Then I heard a voice I knew behind me. "Carolyn, what are you doing here?"

I whirled around to see my husband standing there, a sheepish look on his face and a bloodied rag wrapped around his left hand. "What happened?" I asked as I hugged him.

"I'm fine," he said as he pulled away from me. "Watch the hand, okay?"

"You're bleeding. Why are they making you wait? What did you do to yourself?"

"I had the table-saw blade set a little too high. It's nothing," he said.

"Bleeding like that isn't nothing. Come

on, we're going to get you looked at."

I was ready to unleash on the nurse when she looked up and said, "Bill Emerson."

My husband said, "Wow, you get results."

"Just your husband, ma'am," she said sternly to me.

"If I can't go with him, he's not going in."

"Hey, don't I have a say in this? I really would like somebody to look at this. Go back to your shop. I'll call you when I'm finished."

"You've lost your mind as well, haven't you? I'll be right here when they're finished with you."

He shrugged, then followed the nurse through the forbidden double doors. Before going through, he paused and asked, "How'd you know I was here?"

"A little bird told me. Now go on."

A minute later, David came in. "The parking lot's jammed, so I had to go to the overflow area. How is he?"

"Not nearly as dire as we thought," I said. "He cut his hand on his table saw." The rag he'd wrapped around his hand had been soaked through with blood, but I was hoping it wasn't as serious as it looked. I'd long given up on warning my husband about the dangers of the power equipment he worked with every day. Wood was tougher than flesh, but up until now, he hadn't had an accident. At least not that he'd told me about. "David, why don't you take the car and reopen the shop? There's no telling how long we'll be."

"Sure, I'll be glad to. Listen, I'm sorry if I got you worried over nothing."

I kissed his cheek. "You did exactly the right thing. Now go on. I'll see you soon."

After he was gone, I paced around the waiting room, then sat and picked up one of the year-old magazines lying on a table. I was catching up on old news when I felt a presence in front of me. I looked and was surprised to see Sheriff Hodges standing there.

"What are you doing here?" he asked me.

"I always come here on my lunch hour," I said. "They have the best magazine collection in town."

"Don't be smart with me, Carolyn."

"Bill had an accident," I said.

"Is he all right?" Was that actual concern in the sheriff's voice? Why not? He liked Bill, which was more than he could say about me.

"He seems to think so."

"What happened to him?"

"He cut his hand working on his table saw," I explained.

"They can be nasty things," he replied.

"What brings you here, Sheriff?"

I never thought he'd answer me, but to my surprise, he did. "I'm here checking out an alibi."

"Does it involve someone you suspect in Richard Atkins's murder?" This could be something I could use in my own investigation.

"I'm not at liberty to say," he said, almost by rote.

"Come on, what possible harm could it do?"

"It could give you the false impression that you actually have a right to keep snooping into this when it's none of your business," he said sternly. That was more like the sheriff I knew. His earlier amiable mood had indeed been a fluke.

"The man was killed in my backyard, and I'm the one who tripped over the body. Doesn't that mean anything?"

"I'm sorry you had to find him like that, but that doesn't give you the right to dig into his murder, Carolyn." He tipped his head to me, then left.

I approached the nurse's station and waited patiently until the nurse who had scolded me earlier looked up.

"Yes?"

"I just wanted to say I'm sorry about the way I acted before. I was worried about my husband. I didn't mean to snap at you." I saw one of the other nurses behind the desk smile, but not the woman I was addressing. I was beginning to wonder if her frown was permanently attached.

"Fine. Now take a seat, you're blocking my station."

I looked behind me, but no one was there. "I didn't mean to, but if you've got a second, would you mind telling me what the sheriff wanted? We were talking about checking alibis for one his suspects, but he was called away. I'm sure he wouldn't mind if you told me." That was a whopping big lie, but I was past caring. I needed to know who else was on the sheriff's list of suspects.

"If you want to know, ask him, not me." There was an overhead page, and the nurse I'd been speaking with abruptly turned to the one who had smiled at me and said, "Betty, that's for me. Take over."

After she was gone, I looked at her replacement. "I don't suppose you could help me."

"We're not allowed to give out any information that involves the police. I'm sorry."

"That's all right," I said. I hadn't expected to learn anything, but it hadn't hurt to ask.

I was ready to find a seat again when she said, "You're Carolyn Emerson, aren't you? Don't you run Fire at Will?"

I admitted as much. "Have you ever been in? I don't recognize you."

"No, but I've been meaning to come by. Isn't Rose Colored Glasses near your place?"

"It's just down the River Walk," I said. "Do you shop there?"

"No, I'm new in town. Would you do me a favor? The owner, Rose Nygren, was here a few nights ago, and she left her reading glasses in the waiting area," Betty said. "I've been meaning to return them, but I haven't had the chance. She seems like a nice lady."

"She can be," I said. "I'd be happy to return them for you." As I took the glasses, the magnitude of her words hit home. "Did you say two nights ago?"

"Yes, she brought a friend of hers in to be seen. She must have sat in that waiting room three hours waiting for Mrs. Sampson. Who knows? It could have been longer than that. She was here when my shift started at seven, I know that much."

"Are you saying she was here the entire time?" I asked.

The nurse frowned, then said, "I really couldn't swear to it. Things were kind of crazy that night, so I wasn't keeping tabs on her. But yeah, I think so."

"Thanks," I said as I returned to my seat. Did that mean that Rose had an alibi on the night of the murder? My house was less than five minutes away from the hospital. Did she have time to sneak out, club Richard in my backyard, then make it back here without anyone noticing she was gone? I looked around the room, trying to see if the nurse's station offered a view of the entire waiting area; a few large plants and a television definitely blocked the view. It certainly gave me something to consider. I'd learned earlier that someone had beaten Richard to death, a particularly hideous way to die. How much did you have to hate someone to bludgeon him to death?

I was still pondering the possibilities when I heard Bill's voice. "Are you going with me, or would you like to hang around here all afternoon?"

"What did the doctor say?" I asked as I looked at his hand. It was wrapped in a white bandage held on by a gauze strip two inches wide. A yellow liquid — no doubt, some kind of salve — had discolored part of the bandage.

"I'll be able to play the piano in no time."

"So there's a downside to this," I said.

"Would you be serious for one moment and tell me what happened?"

"Carolyn, when you work with power tools all day, something's bound to happen now and then. It's nothing, not much more than a scratch."

"So he just put some salve on it and wrapped it up?"

"No, the doctor put in a few stitches. Anyway, what makes you think it was a man? My doctor happened to be a very attractive young woman."

"She sounds too good for you," I said curtly.

Bill looked surprised. "Are you honestly mad at me about this?"

"I was sitting out here worried about you, and now I find out you were in there flirting with your physician. Somebody should report her."

"She didn't do anything wrong," Bill said.

"Then they should report you."

"What for, talking to my doctor? Hey, I'm all right," he added softly. "I'm glad you came, but it's going to be fine."

"Let's go home, shall we?" He was right. I wasn't sure why I was snapping at my husband, but I clearly was. "Give me your keys. I'll drive."

"How'd you get here? You didn't walk, did you?"

"Don't be ridiculous. David brought me, then he took the Intrigue back to the shop."

My husband still hesitated.

"Hand them over," I said.

"Thanks, but I'll drive."

"Bill Emerson, I'm perfectly capable of driving that precious truck of yours." Honestly, sometimes I thought he cared more about that vehicle than he did about me.

"It's not that," Bill said. "I want to drop you off at Fire at Will."

"I have no intention of going back to work as if nothing happened," I said.

"That's just it. Nothing did happen, at least nothing deserving this much fuss. Carolyn, I'll call you if I need you, but right now, what I need is some rest. I've got a prescription for the pain, and I think I'll fill it on the way home. The doctor told me they might make me sleepy, which is fine by me. Just because I'm going to take the rest of the day off doesn't mean that you should."

I knew that tone of voice. He didn't want to be pampered, and I'd just end up getting frustrated if I went home with him. I let him drive me to the shop, then hesitated before I got out of the truck. "You'll get your medication, then you're going straight home, right?"

"I promise," he said. "I'm not exactly feeling up to going bowling."

"Call me if you need me," I said.

"You can count on it."

"Bill?"

He had put the truck in gear, but stopped. "Yes?"

"I'm glad it's not worse than it was," I said.

"Me, too," he said with a grin.

I walked inside and found David working on his clay cottage. "How is he?"

"He needed a few stitches, but he's going to be all right."

"You didn't have to come back," David said. "I can handle things here."

"I know you can, but Bill asked me to give him some peace and quiet, so I'm here. Did anything happen while I was gone?"

"Nothing too exciting," he admitted. "A man called here looking for you, but when I told him you were gone, he said he'd check back later."

"How odd. Did he say what he wanted?"

"No, not a word."

"I think I'll make another cottage myself. It's quite fun, isn't it?"

"It's got potential," David admitted.

We were still working side by side when

the door chimed. It was my cottage customer from before, and he had a bittersweet look on his face.

"Did you come back to give me a brochure on skiing this time?" I asked him.

"No, I'm sorry about that. I grabbed the wrong envelope from my jacket pocket."

"I wasn't sure it was an accident," I said. He looked sufficiently contrite, so I decided not to give him a hard time about stiffing me. "What did your mother say?"

"She adored it," he said. "You should have seen her eyes."

"I'm glad she liked it."

He coughed once, then said, "I'd like another, if you don't mind."

"Did something happen to that one?"

"No, but my sister wants one as well."

"How about you?" I asked. "Wouldn't you like one?"

He shook his head sadly. "I'm taking Mother's. We lost her an hour ago."

"I'm so sorry," I said. I hugged him, and he let me.

"Thank you. You've been so kind about the entire thing, I just wanted to come back and tell you how much it meant to her."

"It was my pleasure," I said. How often did I get to give someone their dying wish? "I'm just glad she liked it so much."

"She did." He reached into his jacket and pulled out another envelope. "Sorry about the earlier confusion."

"You don't have to do that," I said, refusing the envelope. "I was happy to help."

"Nonsense. You provided me a wonderful service, and I won't hear of you not taking payment. There's one thing, though."

"What's that?"

"Would you mind terribly if I had that auction leaflet back?"

I'd forgotten all about tacking it to the board behind my register. "Of course not," I said as I retrieved it.

"I'll be back for the cottage in a day or two," he said.

When I looked inside the envelope, four crisp one-hundred-dollar bills looked back.

I started for the door, and David asked, "Is it another brochure?"

"No, but it's too much."

I caught him on the sidewalk, just getting into a Jaguar. "You overpaid me," I said.

"Nonsense. If anything, I didn't give you enough. Please, keep it with my sincere thanks. I'll be offended if you try to return any portion of it."

I grinned. "Well, I wouldn't want that. Thank you."

"I should be the one thanking you," he said.

I walked back inside, and David asked, "What did he say?"

"He told me to keep it."

"Well, the customer's always right," David said with a grin.

"I suppose I'll have to live with it, then." I put the money in the till, then rejoined David at the bench. "Now I need to make another one."

"I thought you already were," he said, pointing down at my clay.

"I've got one already bisque-fired," I admitted, "but I wanted one for the window, too. We should make these to sell."

"Carolyn, not everyone's going to be willing to pay what your last customer did for these things."

"I know that," I said. "But it might make a nice addition to our display."

"Just as long as we don't mass-produce them," David said. "You know how I feel about production work."

I knew all too well. There were two types of potters in the world. One kind, those who had been raised to throw for production, worked incredibly fast and could generate a great deal of stoneware in a short amount of time. The other type, the category that

David fell into, felt that pottery was an art form that should be developed, with careful consideration given to the options each step along the way. I liked both types, for different reasons. Without the production potters, I wouldn't have all of my bisqueware for my paint-your-own customers to enjoy, and without the artistic potters, I wouldn't have some of the breathtakingly beautiful pieces I owned, including some of David's work.

The phone rang, and I answered, "Fire at Will."

"Carolyn, it's Sandy. I was wondering if you'd had a chance to talk to Harvey Jenkins yet."

"As a matter of fact, I did. He claims the ClayDate information dates from when Richard Atkins was in town twenty years ago."

"What? How can that be? I was sure it was more recent than that."

"It's an easy mistake to make," I said. "I shouldn't have rushed you like I did."

"I could have sworn I tapped into the current database," Sandy said. "I feel just awful. I must have made you look like a fool."

"It wasn't that bad," I assured her. "I appreciate your help."

"For all the good it did you. I'm not giving up. I'll keep digging. You can count on me."

"Sandy, it's fine; believe me."

She hung up, and I felt bad about telling her what the mayor had told me. I'd learned that it was easy to run into dead ends investigating without the benefit of the police department's resources. I never would have had the brashness to do it in the first place if I didn't believe that Sheriff Hodges was going to fail to follow all leads in his investigation. I wished the man would just go ahead and retire. Then perhaps we'd get a real sheriff, and I could go back to what I loved to do best, running Fire at Will.

David and I spent the rest of the day making cottages out of clay; a lull in our foot traffic, as happened quite frequently, left us virtually undisturbed. As we loaded the last kiln and turned it on, I asked, "Shall we call it a day? I don't think anybody else is coming in."

"It's fine with me. I've got something I have to do."

"It's not about your father, is it?" I didn't want David going off on his own to investigate.

"I wish everyone would stop calling him that," David said, the irritation thick in his voice. "He walked out on us before I was born, and the first time I laid eyes on him was this week. As far as I'm concerned, he was a stranger, no more, and no less."

"That's kind of callous, isn't it?"

He slammed his hand down, smashing a cottage he'd been working on. "After what he did? You can't be serious."

I couldn't let him go out so angry. It wouldn't do to have the sheriff run into David and get a whiff of the young man's temper. "If you're not doing that, what's this urgent mission?"

He shrugged. "I'm going to talk to Annie. She's got to see that we belong together."

"David, it's her decision as much as it is yours."

He scowled, and whether I liked it or not, I could see some of his father in him. "Carolyn, don't you think I know that? I can't make her want to be with me, but I can at least try to get her back." He looked at me a second, then added, "I'm open to any suggestions you might have."

"I think pleading and groveling couldn't hurt. Also, if you can work it into the conversation up front, tell her what an absolute idiot you've been, and promise her you'll change. But only if you're really willing to."

"I am," he said. "Thanks. How about

flowers? Should I take her some?"

"You've been dating her awhile. What do you think?"

"No, Annie's not one for frills. She'd probably be mad I wasted the money on them."

"Then there's your answer. Good luck, but remember: it's her decision, too, and you should respect whatever she wants."

"You know I will. Mom drilled that into me from the day I could talk."

After he was gone, I closed out the books on the day, turned off the lights, and locked up. It was time to go home and check on my husband. Looking into Richard Atkins's murder would have to wait. I decided to take some of my own advice and put my love life ahead of everything else. Just because Bill and I had been together since dinosaurs roamed the earth didn't mean that I still shouldn't show him how much I cared about him.

CHAPTER 10

Though it was barely seven by the time I got home from work, with a trip to the grocery store thrown in to get some of Bill's favorite foods, my husband was fast asleep; his snoring reverberated through the house. What kind of prescription had they given him? I envied him the sound sleep, but not the pain he must be feeling. Though he'd protested that it hadn't been that bad, I knew my husband. That cut had hurt, and not just his pride, which was considerable. He fancied himself an accomplished woodworker, and he was — that was easy to see in the beautiful pieces he made — but even pros had accidents. I saw it as a mark of his skill that it had taken this long for him to have an injury that drew enough blood to require stitches.

I'd planned to make him his favorite dinner, homemade chili hot enough to blow the top of his head off. Even though he was sleeping, I decided there wasn't any harm in making it now. I'd simmer it on the stove, and when he woke up from this drug-induced nap, a bowl of it would be waiting for him.

I made two batches, a big one for him full of spicy additions, and something a little more bland for me, though it was still hot enough to bring tears to my eyes. As both pots simmered on the stove, I looked in on him again. He hadn't even shifted his position on the bed. It didn't make sense for me to wait to eat with him, since it could be hours until he woke, and I was hungry now. I dished out some of the milder blend, cut off a chunk of sharp cheddar cheese, grabbed some crackers and a cold glass of milk, then set a place at the table and ate. The meal was fine, but I missed my husband, even though he was just in the other room. Was this how it was for my friends who had lost their spouses through death or divorce? I wondered how many meals Jenna, a widow, had eaten alone. How did she stand it? I'd have to be a better friend and invite her over more often than I did, which was hardly ever.

After I ate, I cleaned up, took Bill's pot of chili off the stove, and mulled over what to do next. Television didn't interest me, and I wasn't in the mood to read. I was still upset about somebody murdering Richard Atkins in my backyard, but I wasn't going to let them drive me from my land. I grabbed my coat, jotted a quick note to Bill, and propped it up beside his awaiting bowl. Then I walked outside, grabbing the flashlight by the back door as I left.

It was a crisp evening, and the moon was full and bright, obscured only occasionally by scudding clouds. I loved our property, especially the way the land went back into the woods behind us. It gave me the illusion that we abutted some great, wild wilderness, though I knew the next street over was just a hundred yards away. I thought Bill had been foolishly extravagant when he'd bought the abutting lots along with our property, but I had seen his wisdom a thousand times since. While our neighbors were surrounded by each other, we had the luxury of space around us, something that I cherished.

I found myself drawn to my raku pit for the first time since I'd stumbled across the body. The police tape was gone, and there was honestly no indication that something dire had ever happened there. As I stared at the pit where I buried the pots freshly removed from the gas kiln beside it, I began to wonder something that should have piqued my interest from the start. What on earth had Richard been doing in my backyard in the first place? Did it have anything to do with him abandoning his car practically in my driveway the night before he was murdered? It was an odd place for a rendezvous, that was for sure.

I'd asked Bill about putting a security light in back so we could see if someone was out there, but my husband had protested that a light would just make it easier for a burglar to see what he was doing. Why help him break into our house?

I heard a noise in the woods in front of me, but the flashlight beam was too weak to penetrate very far into the darkness. I knew raccoons frequently ran through the woods, and neighborhood cats came and went as well. I'd just about decided that whatever it was had left when I heard a branch crack. From the sound of it, this was no raccoon. For once, my survival instinct was solid, and I raced back to the house, dropping the flashlight as I ran. There was enough moonlight to show the way, and the light I'd left on in the kitchen was like a beacon drawing me home. My heart was racing when I got back inside, but I didn't slow down until the door was safely dead-bolted behind me.

"What happened? Did you see a ghost?"

My husband was sitting at the kitchen table, polishing off the bowl of the chili I'd left him.

"No, it was nothing. I just decided to go for a walk out back. How's your hand?"

He flexed it slightly. "It's better. That medication knocked me out. Sorry about that."

"Sleep has to be good for you," I said. "Did you enjoy your chili?"

"I still am." He smiled as he took another bite. I sat across from him, happy that he was awake. "Thanks for this."

"You're most welcome. I thought you might like some comfort food tonight."

He stared at his hand. "It's not that bad, really."

"I know. Accidents happen."

He searched my eyes and saw no sarcasm in them. I heard his sigh of relief as he realized I wasn't going to say anything about what had happened.

"Maybe I'm getting too old for this foolishness," Bill said.

"You don't have to keep making furniture," I said, "but I know how much you love it. You shouldn't let this stop you. In fact, I think you should get back to it as soon as you're able."

He shook his head. "The doctor told me to lay off until I've finished my prescription. It makes me kind of loopy."

"I didn't mean tonight," I said. "But don't let this stop you for good."

He nodded. "I have to admit, it was scary looking down and seeing that blood."

"Did it hurt when the blade hit your hand?"

He rubbed his chin with his good hand. "No, as a matter of fact, it didn't. It took me a few seconds to even realize that I'd been cut. Seeing the blood was what triggered the pain." He shook his head briefly. "The medication's taking care of it right now." He pushed his bowl away. "That was perfect. Carolyn, I hate to be this way, but I think I'm going back to bed."

"That's a splendid idea," I said. "When are you due to take more medication?"

"I've got another half an hour." He winced slightly. "Do you think it would hurt to speed it up a little bit?"

"As long as you don't make a habit of it," I said. "Let me get it for you."

"That's all right. I've got it on the nightstand. I'll see you in the morning."

I kissed him quickly, then said, "Sleep tight."

"With this stuff? That's not going to be a

216

problem, believe me."

It wasn't even nine yet, too early for me to go to bed. As Bill's snoring reached a particularly loud level of buzz-sawing, I thought about making up the spare bedroom and bunking in there for the night. No, then I wouldn't be nearby if my husband needed me, and that was more important than a sound night's sleep. I sat in the living room for an hour or so, doing not much of anything and had just about decided to turn in myself when I heard a tapping at the front door. Who on earth would come visiting this late? I flicked on the porch light and looked out the peephole, prepared to ignore whoever had come by.

I changed my mind and opened the door the second I saw who it was.

"Come in," I told Hannah. "What's going on?"

"I didn't wake you, did I?"

"No, but Bill's already asleep."

She looked uncomfortable. "This can wait."

"Hannah, he's on medication for his hand. I doubt he'd hear us if we started a drum and bugle corps."

She didn't come in. "I hadn't heard. What happened to him?"

"There was a little accident in his shop," I

said lightly, trying to disguise how I really felt about it. "He needed a few stitches, and he's on something for the pain. You've saved me from endless boredom. Now are you coming in, or should I join you outside?"

"I'll come in, but I'm just going to stay a minute."

"How's tea sound?" I said as I closed the door behind her and bolted it. "I'm in the mood for some Darjeeling."

"I'll take anything but iced," she said. "It's really getting chilly out there."

"Why don't you come back into the kitchen with me and we can chat while I put the kettle on."

She joined me in the kitchen, and as I filled up my burnished copper teakettle, Hannah said, "I didn't think anyone made tea on a stove top anymore."

"There are a few of us relics still out there," I said.

"Carolyn, I didn't mean anything by it."

I laughed as I said, "I know you didn't. I was joking myself. I know I can just as easily microwave the water, but there's something safe and reassuring about a teakettle, don't you think?"

"I never thought about it before," she said, "but I suppose you're right."

"If nothing else, it's a great deal more fun

than a microwave." I rummaged through my cabinets until I found the tin with Darjeeling in it. It was awfully light, even for a container with tea leaves. My fears were realized when I saw that I was nearly out. "Okay, no Darjeeling. I've got a jasmine blend, and some sassafras tea as well. I know I have both of those."

"I haven't had sassafras since I was a little girl," Hannah said. "Isn't it bad for you?"

"This has been processed, so it's high time you revisit it. You still like licorice, don't you?"

"Occasionally," she admitted, "though I'm afraid I haven't had that in ages, either."

"Then you're in for a real treat." I pulled the sassafras chunks from the freezer where I kept them and dropped some in the kettle. "Now, let's see, I've got some cookies around here somewhere."

"Carolyn, I don't need a snack. Would you sit down here with me? There's something we need to talk about."

"That sounds serious," I said. "Perhaps it should wait until after our tea is ready."

"I suppose," she agreed. I was in no hurry for the kettle to whistle. Hannah was visibly upset, and I was almost certain it had something to do with Richard Atkins.

Impatiently, she said, "You know what? I

can't wait for the kettle to boil. I'm here to talk about David."

"What about him?" I asked as the kettle began to whistle. "The sheriff didn't arrest him after all, did he?"

"No, at least he hadn't half an hour ago when I left him. This is about Annie."

I reached for the kettle and strained two mugs of tea. The sassafras had a strong licorice smell to it, and to be honest, I kept it just as much for the mildly sweet aroma it gave off as I did to drink the brew.

"I've made it a point to stay out of David's love life," I said as I handed Hannah a mug.

"Well, you're not his mother," she replied.

"No, but I care about him, and I hate to see him get hurt as much as anybody does, with the possible exception of you."

"I know, excuse me for being so snippy. He's just devastated this girl has broken his heart."

I looked at her closely. "Have you talked to him today?"

"No, that's the problem. He was mooning all over the house last night, and now he hasn't even come home. I'm worried sick about him."

"He's a grown man, Hannah. The last time I saw him, he was going to try to win her back. Have you considered the possibility that he was successful, and that they're together right now?"

"Which is worse?" she asked softly, most likely thinking I hadn't heard.

"If you have to ask that, you're not the mother you think you are. Hannah, you can't keep him your baby boy forever. He has the right to a life of his own. Look, don't borrow trouble. Wait to hear what he has to say before you condemn him for something he may not have even done."

I don't think she could have looked any more shocked if I'd slapped her. With an expression devoid of all emotion, she put the mug down and left, without a peep, a whimper, or a single word. Perhaps I'd gone too far at last. This might be the breach that couldn't be fixed with club sandwiches or tea. But the words needed to be said, and Hannah needed to hear them. Suddenly I was very tired, of everything. What I needed now was rest, and time to lock the world away.

With the collection of nightmares I had, I might as well have stayed awake. Bill's snoring beside me didn't help matters, though I couldn't say it hurt all that much, either.

After my restless night, I wasn't ready to

face a new day when my alarm went off, but I didn't have much choice.

Bill was annoyingly refreshed as he popped up beside me. "That was some night. How'd you sleep?" he asked as he practically leapt out of bed.

"Barely," I said.

"Really? I had a great rest. My hand's not even that sore. I think I'll go back to the shop today."

"Don't you think you should take a little more time off? You don't want to rush it, and if you even get near those pills, I won't allow any woodworking. Do you understand?"

Normally my scolding would set him off, but not today. "I don't need them, I tell you. Maybe tonight, though." The grin on his lips made me uneasy.

"Pain pills are the easiest thing in the world to get addicted to," I said. "Easier than heroin, alcohol, or cocaine." I wasn't entirely sure that was true, but I didn't want my husband hooked on the medication. That wasn't the whole story, though. For some reason, my dear spouse was aggravating the fool out of me, and I felt the need to come down hard on him.

"Hey, I'm the one who said I was done with them, remember? If I don't hurt, I don't need them, and I won't take any more."

"That's a slippery slope, and you know it. Tell you what. Why don't I hang on to them for you."

"I'm not a child, Carolyn. I'm perfectly capable of dispensing my own medication. I'm going to go take a shower," he said grumpily.

I felt a twinge of guilt about crushing his good mood. But I was still upset with his jaunty attitude. Out of aggravation more than anything else, I stole into the bedroom and put his bottle of pills by the cleaning supplies in the kitchen. He'd never look there; I had full confidence in that. If he asked, I'd turn them back over to him, but he was going to have to make the request.

After he got out of the shower, he didn't mention the pills again, and I certainly wasn't going to bring it up. I made us eggs for breakfast, and he headed back to his workshop.

Or so I thought.

"Carolyn, you might want to come out here," he said as he called to me from the back porch.

"What happened, did another dog make a deposit on our deck?" Some of the neighborhood dogs loved leaving us little presents, and Bill had threatened to electrify the entire place on more than one occasion.

"No, it's nothing like that. Come out here. Now."

"All right, I'm coming. There's no need to be so gruff about it," I said as I joined him outside.

The second I got outside, I saw what had disturbed him so. Someone had scrawled the words "BUTT OUT" on my car windshield in big block letters with a black Sharpie pen.

"That's rather clear, isn't it?" I said.

"Who did this?" Bill asked. "Do you have any idea?"

"It could have been a dozen different people," I said, more honestly than I wanted to admit.

"I'm going to call the sheriff," Bill said as he started back inside.

I grabbed his sleeve, being careful not to touch his hand. "Don't, Bill. It's not going to do any good."

"He needs to be told someone's threatening you," Bill said, shaking off my grip.

"Let me deal with it in my own way," I said. I couldn't imagine Hannah writing such a terse message, but she'd been angrier than I'd ever seen her in my life. I couldn't rule it out, not completely.

"Are you at least going to take the advice?" he asked.

"What do you think?"

"I think I wasted my breath even asking you the question," he said as he started to walk away.

"Where are you going?" I asked.

"If you're not going to let me call the sheriff, I'm going to my workshop."

He stormed off to his shop and went inside. It was a hundred feet from my raku pit, on the other edge of our property line, and I wondered if my woodlands visitor might have done something to my husband's shop. He didn't come back out, so I had to assume it was undisturbed.

I went back into the house, grabbed the phone, then stared at it a full minute before I had the nerve to dial the number I had to call.

"Yes?" Hannah said, her voice full of frost.

"It's me," I said. "I want to talk to you about what happened last night."

"There's nothing to talk about," she said.

"You didn't leave me any messages, did you?" There, I'd said it.

"I haven't called you. Why would you think I had?"

"I'm not talking about on the telephone. I mean on my windshield."

"Carolyn, what on earth are you talking about?"

"I didn't think you'd do it," I said.

"What was the message?"

I had to tell her. "It said 'butt out.' "

"I can understand the sentiment, but I didn't leave the message," she said, and then she hung up.

That answered that. I knew Hannah well enough to know that if she'd done it, she would have at least admitted it to me. So, who else wanted me to mind my own business? It could have been a message from Rose Nygren, Kendra Williams, Mayor Harvey Jenkins, or my uncle Don Rutledge. Then again, it could have been half a dozen other people I didn't even realize I'd offended with my impromptu investigation. Whoever it was, they were going to have to do better than that to get me to stop.

If anything, I was more determined than ever to find out what had happened to Richard Atkins in my raku pit, and just as important, why.

Butch Hardcastle was waiting for me in front of the shop when I got there thirty minutes later. He handed me a cup of coffee. "I thought you could use this."

"How did you know I didn't meet Hannah this morning?" Was the man watching me?

"I didn't. Here, give it back and I'll drink it."

"Not on your life," I said. "I need this."

"Two cups already? I don't want to be the one responsible for you getting the jitters."

I opened the door and let him in. "As a matter of fact, Hannah and I skipped our morning ritual," I said as I dead-bolted the door behind us.

"Are you two squabbling again?" he asked.

"I'm afraid I might have pushed things a little too far this time." I told him what I'd said to Hannah about David and waited for his reaction. All he did was listen. "No comment?"

"Are you kidding? I've got enough problems without getting involved in a fight between two strong-willed women. No, I'll stay on the sidelines for this one."

I snorted. "A fat lot of help you are, then. So, what brings you here so early? I wouldn't think you'd be up at this hour."

He grinned. "I've found it's a whole lot easier if you don't go to bed first."

"You've been up all night? My mother always told me nothing good happens after midnight."

Butch pulled up a chair and sat down.

"Then we wouldn't have had much in common. Sometimes I think just the opposite is true."

I grabbed a seat across from him. "Butch, you haven't been backsliding, have you?"

He patted my hand. "Carolyn, I appreciate your concern, honestly, I do, but I'm a big boy. I can take care of myself."

"I know you can. I just worry about you sometimes. I can't help it, so don't ask me to stop."

"I won't," he said. "I'm here this early for a reason."

"Not just my company? I figured as much. What's up?"

He reached into his pocket and pulled out a folded envelope. "I may have found something about Richard Atkins's first disappearance." He slid the envelope across the table to me. "See what you think."

Inside was a faded and yellowed newspaper article, and it broke in two as I unfolded it. "Sorry about that."

"That's all right. Read it."

Holding the pieces together, I scanned the article, then looked up. "It's about a jewelry store robbery. I remember reading about it back then." In fact, Kendra had brought up the subject when she'd first heard that Richard had returned to Maple Ridge.

"Look at the date," he said as he tapped the paper.

"Okay. It doesn't have much significance to me. I'm sorry, I must be a little slow this morning."

Butch sighed. "Think about it. You know David's birthday, don't you?"

"Of course I do. It's March eleventh."

"You know the year as well, I'll wager. Take that date, count back seven months, and what have you got? I imagine it's about the time Hannah knew she was pregnant with him."

I frowned at him. "Are you saying that the two events are related? Do you honestly believe Richard Atkins found out his wife was pregnant, then decided to go out and rob a jewelry store to celebrate? The owner was shot and wounded. It hardly seems the proper way to celebrate."

"I don't believe in coincidences, Carolyn. This has to be related."

"But how?"

"Give me some time. I'll dig into it and get back to you. But first I've got to go out of town today."

As we stood, I said, "I'm not even going to bother asking you where you're going."

He smiled. "Good. Then I won't have to lie to you. If you're in a hurry for the information, it won't hurt my feelings if you look into this yourself."

"I've got a better idea. Why don't I ask Sandy?"

"That works for me. I'll stop by when I get back into town."

I couldn't let him go yet. I held his hands in mine, then said, "Be careful. Promise me that much."

"Yes, ma'am."

Once he was gone, I dialed Sandy's number at the library. Before I could tell her what I wanted her to investigate, she said, "Carolyn, I haven't had a chance to look into that ClayDate thing since we spoke yesterday. Things have been kind of crazy around here."

"That's fine." It looked as though I was going to have to research the robbery myself.

Before I could hang up, she asked, "That was why you were calling, wasn't it?"

"No, but it can wait."

"You can't tease me like that," she said. "I'll fret about it all day."

I quickly relayed Butch's hunch to her, expecting her to dismiss it out of hand. Instead she said, "I can get back to you in half an hour."

"I thought you were busy," I said.

"I've got time for this. It's an entirely different kind of search. This is all open information. Will you be at the shop this morning?"

"Who knows? I think so, but that's no real indication, given the way my days have been going lately."

"I'll track you down, then," she said, and then hung up.

David wasn't due in for an hour yet, and though I had a hundred things I could do, I didn't want to do any of them. Was I losing my drive for running Fire at Will? No, I still loved working with clay, glaze, and paint. It was just that I had so many distractions to deal with, I couldn't enjoy my real purpose in life.

I decided to open my kilns to see how the cottages had turned out. As I unloaded them, I marveled at the simple little structures, and how much fun they were to make. Though they were all the reddish pink of bisque-fired clay, I could imagine the many variations we could make with paint and glaze. Taking one of the cottages I'd created, I sat down at one of the painting benches and lost myself in decorating the structure. When I looked up from my work, I saw that I should have opened my door twenty minutes earlier. I'd been so wrapped up in what I'd been doing that the time had flown past me. As I unlocked the door, I was a little disgruntled that no eager customers had brought my tardiness to my attention.

I'd just flipped the sign on the front door when David came trotting up. "Sorry I'm late. I slept in."

"Is that good news, or bad? Did you have any luck with Annie?"

"She's thawing, but it's still kind of chilly," he admitted as he took off his jacket and hung it on a peg. "Speaking of arctic blasts, I talked to my mom this morning."

"Did you? What did she have to say for herself?"

He whistled. "I thought I was the only one in the world who could push her buttons like that, but you must have found a few I didn't even know existed. You probably should know that you're not one of her favorite people in the world right now."

"I didn't think I was," I said as I returned to my cottage. I'd suddenly lost interest in working on it, but it was nearly finished. It had been for ten minutes, but I'd been enjoying adding little details, like a black cat perched on the front stoop. The next house I did would have a three-dimensional feline on it. I had a core group of customers who would buy anything I made as long as it had a cat on it. The only catch was, it had to be unique, so I was constantly searching for more ways to add cats to my pieces. I loved them myself, but it was strictly a marketing decision. Okay, that wasn't true. They were fun to do, and I considered it a challenge making the felines fit in.

"Do you want to talk about it?" David asked as he put on his apron.

"That's the last thing I want to do," I said. "Let's finish these cottages, shall we? I want to get them fired and in the window as fast as I can."

"We're not doing production work, are we?"

"No, but if these little buildings help pay the rent, we should embrace them."

"Okay, I get it," he said. As he looked at the pieces spread out on a table by the kilns, David said, "We've got a lot of work to do."

"I think we should just glaze half of them," I said. "We can put the others out on the open shelves for our customers."

"Have you thought about what you're going to charge for them?"

"Not yet," I said. "For now, just put them in the most expensive pricing section and we'll figure out an exact amount later."

I had my shelves of bisqueware organized,

from the least expensive saucers to the fanciest jugs and teakettles. The system wasn't perfect, but it was the best I'd been able to come up with in the years I'd owned Fire at Will. Pricing the pieces I bought wholesale wasn't that difficult. But David liked to add his own work to the shelves, and Robert Owens, the potter from Travers who sometimes taught classes at the shop, often put the pieces he didn't think were quite good enough on the shelves, too. I hadn't seen him lately, because he was on some kind of research trip in Europe — nice work if you could get it. I seemed to be stuck in Maple Ridge. Not that I didn't love our little corner of Vermont, but sometimes I got the itch to grab my husband, get the next flight out, and see what the world had to offer. The funny thing was, I knew if we ever actually did it, in three or four days I'd be yearning for my kilns and pottery again. It was something that drove my husband crazy, but I couldn't help myself.

I saw David holding one of the cottages he'd made. "Are you going to do that one for the window?"

"No, I thought I'd keep this one myself. You don't mind, do you?"

"Of course not. Is it going to be a gift?"

He grinned. "It might be. It depends on

how well things go later, I guess."

"You could always give it to your mother."

"Or you could make one for her yourself as a peace gesture."

I looked sharply at him. "David, I thought we weren't going to talk about that."

"Hey, don't blame me. You're the one who brought her up."

I wasn't about to argue, especially since he was right. "Are we going to decorate these or not?"

"I'm right behind you."

We quickly lapsed into our old habits of conversation as we worked on our pieces side by side. Business at the shop was slow, but at least David and I were doing something productive with our time. Summer would be upon us soon enough, and we wouldn't have much opportunity to work on our own projects. Still, I was a little concerned about the lull in revenue.

When Sandy came in, I forgot all about those concerns. The look of sheer exuberance on her face could mean only one thing. She'd uncovered something she thought was significant in the case.

CHAPTER 11

"Can we talk?" Sandy asked me, her eyes darting quickly to David.

"I won't tell, I promise," David said. "You can say whatever you want to in front of me."

"Don't be that way," I told David. "This might not concern you. Why don't you take an early lunch? Don't worry about the mess. I'll clean it up."

"In that case, be my guest. Sandy, you can come by the shop any time." He washed up, traded his apron for his jacket, and then David was gone.

"Sorry about that," Sandy said as soon as the door closed. "I just didn't think it was right talking about his father in front of him."

"So you found something else?" I asked.

"I'm not sure if there's any fire, but I'm close enough to something to smell smoke."

"Well, don't hold out on me. What is it?"

"I didn't get this on the Internet. My boss Corki gave me the scoop about what happened. She was married to one of Hodges's deputies around the time that Richard left town."

I knew Corki had gone through a pair of dud husbands before she'd found a keeper, but we hadn't been friends back then. "What did she say?"

"It's about the jewelry store robbery. The police believed two men were in on the theft, though that never made it into the papers. They never had any idea who one of them was, but they were looking hard at one of our prominent citizens as the accomplice. Harvey Jenkins opened up his first car dealership around then, and it wasn't entirely clear where he got his backing."

"Did your boss actually say the mayor of Maple Ridge is a thief?"

Sandy shook her head. "No, apparently Harvey had an alibi, but that doesn't mean he wasn't in on it. And there's something else."

"Go on," I said. For a reference librarian — someone who made her living telling people things they wanted to know — Sandy sure seemed to enjoy ratcheting up the suspense.

237

"Corki's ex also interviewed Richard Atkins. They couldn't find any hard evidence against him, but not long after the robbery, he left town, so it made the police wonder."

"That's what Butch thought, but I'm still not convinced."

"Here's the part where it gets worse," Sandy said. "The jewelry store owner who was shot and wounded died a few years after the robbery. They say he was never the same after what happened."

"How does that fit into the rest of this?"

"He was Annie Gregg's dad," Sandy said.

"That would give her a motive for killing Richard, if he had been involved and she knew it," I said.

"And if that's true, then the mayor better watch his back as well."

I tried to picture the sweet young woman I knew doing something so cold-blooded. "No," I said after a moment, "I can't believe Annie would have anything to do with what happened to Richard. She's not that kind of girl."

"What, the kind who kills to revenge her father? Face it, Carolyn, it's hard to say who would or wouldn't be capable of that, isn't it? I'm sorry I don't have more, but there was really nothing official ever filed. As far as I know, the case is still open."

"You've given me plenty to think about," I said.

"Well, I'd better get back to the library, but I wanted to tell you what I'd heard as soon as I could."

"Thanks," I said as Sandy hurried out.

Was it possible that Annie had been dating the son of the man who'd killed her father? Could that, rather than David's behavior, have spurred the break up? I found it difficult to imagine Annie killing anybody, but Sandy was right. Who knew what a person was capable of, given the right circumstances.

I was still mulling over what Sandy had told me when David poked his head in through the front door. "Is it safe to come back in?"

"The coast is clear," I said, trying to lighten my dire mood. "How was lunch?"

"It was good," he said. "I called Annie and she actually agreed to have a bite with me. I think there's a glimmer of hope there somewhere."

"Hope is a wonderful thing, isn't it?" I couldn't exactly warn David that his girlfriend might be a killer, but could I just let it go? Evidently not. "You're sure you're doing the right thing with Annie, right?"

"What do you mean, Carolyn?"

I really was out of line, especially if Sandy was wrong about Annie's actions. Whatever happened to being innocent until proven guilty? "Don't listen to me. I'm just an old poop sometimes."

He shrugged, dismissing it. "Are you ready to do some more decorating?"

"What I'm ready for is my lunch, young man. Watch the shop. I'll see you soon." I grabbed my coat and got out of there. Until I was sure about Annie, I had to watch what I said around David. I didn't want to poison his chance at love if my suspicions were unfounded.

"Annie, it's Carolyn Emerson. Do you have a minute?" I figured the best place to get information about the girl was to go directly to the source. At least I'd remembered to charge my cell phone, so I could make this call in the relative privacy of a bench overlooking the brook.

"Hi, Carolyn. I just took my lunch break with David, and it put me behind. Sorry."

"This won't take long," I promised. "All I need is five minutes. I can come to you, if you'd like."

She paused, then said, "No, I can meet you. Are you at the shop?"

"Actually, I'm getting ready to go to Shelly's. I know you've eaten, but how about some pie?"

"Please, I'm getting plump as it is. David loves to eat out, and I've been gaining weight from the moment we met."

"Okay, no pie. What about coffee? We could meet at In the Grounds."

"I suppose so. Carolyn, there's no chance we can do this right now over the telephone, is there?"

"I think it would be better face-to-face," I said.

"If you say so. I'll see you soon."

I hurried over to the coffee shop, securing a table by the window where I could watch for her. Nate Walker, the owner of the place, approached.

"Hi, Carolyn. I was beginning to think you'd forgotten we were here. Are you and Hannah fighting?"

"What makes you ask that?"

"Come on, I can set my watch by you two, but lately, neither one of you has been coming by. I'm beginning to wonder if it was something I said."

"It's not you, it's us. I'd like two coffees, please."

He looked out the window. "Does that mean Hannah's going to join you?"

"No, this one's for someone else."

He nodded gravely, then left to get my order. Twenty seconds after the coffee was delivered, Annie arrived. I was struck again by how much Annie resembled the actress Julia Roberts. It was easy to see why David had found her attractive, but I knew Annie's charms went far beyond her appearance.

"Thanks for the coffee," she said as she took a sip.

"Don't you even want to know what I ordered for you?" I asked, smiling.

"If it's got caffeine, we're good," she said. "I was up pretty late last night."

"So I heard," I said without realizing how it must have sounded. "Sorry about that. I didn't mean to butt in."

"It's fine. I fully expected David to talk to you about our situation. I know you two are very close."

"We are. I'd hate to see him get hurt," I said, refraining from adding any more to that statement.

"I don't want to hurt him, believe me. I care for David." I could see in her eyes that it was true.

"His father's sudden reappearance was pretty shocking, wasn't it?" I said.

"I guess. It's been hard on him all these years not having a dad."

"The same can be said for you, can't it? You two have a great deal in common in that regard," I said. Then I sipped my coffee.

"It's true. I never knew my father, either," she admitted. "Somebody stole that from me."

"What an unusual way to put it."

For an instant, she looked furious. "How else would you say it? That robber killed him, just as surely as if he'd put that gun to my dad's head and pulled the trigger again."

"It sounds like the wound is still raw for you." Annie's emotions were breaking through her normally happy demeanor.

"Carolyn, what was so urgent that we had to meet? I don't have much time."

"It's about David," I said.

I was still struggling for words when Annie said, "No offense, but I'm not sure it's any of your business. I know you two are close, but you're not his mother, and I wouldn't even be discussing this with her, if she cared enough to ask."

"Hannah loves him a great deal," I said softly.

"There's got to be room in his life for someone else." She threw two ones on the table. "I've got to go."

I picked up the bills and tried to hand

them back to her. "This was my treat."

"Thanks, but I pay my own way."

After she was gone, I stared at my coffee. Suddenly, I wasn't nearly as sure as I had been that Annie wasn't involved in the murder. If she suspected that Richard had committed that robbery twenty years ago, I doubted she would hesitate to exact her revenge. Whether or not I liked it, I was going to have to add her to my list of suspects.

"May I join you? All the other tables are full." I looked up to see Mayor Jenkins standing in front of me.

I moved Annie's cup to my side and motioned to a seat. "Help yourself."

He nodded, then settled in across from me. Harvey Jenkins was fighting his spreading waistline, and was obviously losing. His clothes, while nicely cut, were too young for a man his age, as was his fancy haircut. He looked like a man trying to hold on to something that was long gone.

"Listen, I'm sorry about our earlier conversation during your test drive. You caught me at a bad time."

"We all have them," I said. "Don't worry about it." Clearly, he was trying to put our earlier encounter behind him. I wasn't sure I was going to let him, but I'd see what he had to say.

"You're looking a little ragged around the edges, Carolyn," he said. "Are you getting enough sleep?"

"My, you know just what to say to turn a woman's head," I answered. "No wonder you keep getting reelected."

He smiled. "Granted, that was probably a little harsh." He stifled a yawn. "I had a rather late night myself. A mayor's work is never done. I keep pushing for it to be a full-time job, but so far, nobody wants that but me."

"You'd miss your dealership, wouldn't you? I'm sure you make a killing off it."

He raised one eyebrow. "You'd be surprised. How's the pottery business?"

"We're getting by," I said. "Actually, I had an interesting conversation about you this morning."

Harvey rubbed his ears. "I thought I felt my ears burning. Only good, I hope."

"That depends. We were talking about the robbery twenty years ago at Quality Jewelry."

Did I see a flinch when I mentioned the name of the store? "How on earth was my name tied to that?" Harvey asked, seemingly perplexed.

"We were discussing things that happened around the time Richard Atkins took off.

The jewelry store robbery and the opening of your first car dealership all happened at about the same time, didn't they?"

"It was a long time ago," he said. "I'm sure they weren't all that close together. The years have a tendency to blend together, don't they?" He sipped his coffee, but the mayor's gaze never left my face. If nothing else, I'd certainly managed to pique his curiosity. "Who exactly were you discussing all this with, your husband?"

"No, Bill was already at work by then. It's a small world, isn't it?"

"And getting smaller by the minute," he said as he looked over my shoulder. "Thanks for the seat, but a booth just opened up."

"Don't rush off on my account," I said.

"Of course not. I've just got a few calls to make while I drink my coffee, and it would be rude to do that in front of you. Good bye."

"I'll see you later," I said.

I'd delayed my lunch hour long enough, but I didn't want to eat at the coffee shop. Neither did I feel like going under Shelly's microscope, so instead, on a whim I got into the Intrigue and drove home.

Bill's truck was parked in the driveway, and I was happy he was home. My husband wasn't the most romantic man in the world;

in fact, much of the time he could be downright gruff. But something about his presence soothed me, made me feel safe, like I belonged. I'd never tried to convey that in words to him, and even if I did I doubted he'd understand. But that didn't matter. I knew, and that was enough.

"Bill? Are you in here?" No answer. He must still be in his shop, though with his injured hand, I wondered how much work he'd be able to accomplish.

I walked out through the back door and started for his woodworking shop. As I walked, I noticed something odd about the backyard. The lawn was filled with small holes and looked as though it'd been invaded by a horde of gophers. Bill wasn't all that keen on landscaping, and neither was I, but I was sure we couldn't allow this rampage to go unchecked.

I finally found him in his shop leafing through plan books. "What's going on?" I asked.

"Carolyn? What in the world are you doing here? Why aren't you at work?"

"I thought I'd come home to see my husband. That's allowed, isn't it?" He didn't look all that pleased to see me.

"You know it is. I just thought you'd be

too busy. You don't usually pop home for lunch."

"Listen, if I've interrupted some grand plans of yours, I can make a quick sandwich and take it back to the pottery shop with me." I'd had warmer welcomes at my dentist's office.

"I'm sorry," he said abruptly. "This blasted hand hurts too much when I try to do anything, and if I take a pill for the pain, I'm too loopy to work. I can't win."

"So why are you sitting out here feeling sorry for yourself?"

"I don't have the slightest idea," he said, trying to scare up a smile but managing only a sickly grin.

"Come on in and I'll make something for both of us." I offered him my hand, and he took it.

"That's the best idea I've had all day."

"I believe it was mine."

"Don't quibble. What's for lunch?"

I thought about what I had in my refrigerator and freezer, and realized a real shopping trip to the grocery store was long past due. "Let's go see, shall we?"

As we walked back to the house, I said, "The gophers are getting pretty aggressive with our backyard. There are lumps everywhere."

"Fine," he said absentmindedly.

"I was thinking about getting some dynamite and taking care of it myself."

"That's good," he said, still lost in thoughts of his own. "Wait a second. Did you say dynamite?"

"I did indeed."

"There's no need for anything that drastic," he said.

"Don't scold me. I was just trying to see if you were paying any attention to me, which you weren't."

"I've got deadlines to meet, Carolyn. This is serious."

I stopped at the door and turned to Bill. "You are retired. Stop acting like you have to earn a living, because you don't. We're fine. If you have to, give back the money you took as a down payment."

He pulled away from me. "It's not the money, and you know it. I gave my word, and now I'm not going to be able to keep it. You know how I feel about that."

"You can't heal yourself," I said, suddenly angry. "The harder you push, the longer it's going to take you to get better."

"I keep telling you, it's not that bad."

"It's serious enough to keep you from working. Do you really want to have this argument again?"

"No, not particularly," he said gruffly.

"Then let's find something to eat."

I poked around the kitchen, but the supplies were low in nearly every department. "How about an omelet?" I asked.

"For lunch?"

"No, I'm thinking about breakfast three weeks from Thursday. Do you think you'll be in the mood for one then? I can pencil it in, then you can change your mind if you'd like."

He looked surprised. "There's no need to snap."

"Then don't ask silly questions. I'm not in the mood for it. Is it going to be eggs, or would you prefer peanut butter sandwiches?"

He smiled, then said, "Eggs sound fine."

"Just fine?" I was in a snit, and I couldn't do anything about it. It would wear off eventually, but for the moment, I couldn't seem to stop myself from snapping at my husband.

"Grand, wondrous, joyful, delightful. That's what I meant to say."

I stared at him for ten seconds, then returned his smile. "Eggs it is."

"I'll do the toast," he volunteered, "and I'll grate the cheese, too. Let's make omelets."

"You're a model of helpfulness," I said.

"Are you kidding? I'm afraid if I don't, you won't feed me at all."

I put the pan down, but before I cracked the eggs, I said, "Bill, I am sorry. I know I'm being a little abrasive, but this murder is digging up things that might be better off left buried."

"You don't have to investigate it yourself, you know."

"I can't just let it go," I said as I rinsed the eggs and cracked them open. As I put them in a bowl and stirred in some milk, I added, "It's not in my nature."

"I know. It was just a suggestion. What are we going to do with ourselves? I'm a wood-worker who can't use his shop, and you're a shop owner who doesn't have time for her business. We're quite the pair, aren't we?"

"I like us, despite our varied flaws," I said.

"So do I." He hugged me briefly, then said, "I'll have that cheese for you in a minute."

I made the omelet big enough for both of us, and it was delicious, especially with the sharp cheddar cheese we both preferred.

After we ate, Bill pushed his plate away. "What's for dessert?"

"Do you have to have something sweet after every meal?"

He shrugged. "I don't have to, but it sure tastes good."

"There's one slice left of the lemon meringue pie, but I thought you were saving it for tonight."

"Forget that. Grab two forks and I'll split it with you."

"I'd better not," I said. "I've got to get back to Fire at Will. I've left David there long enough."

"Suit yourself," he said, happily sliding out the pie tin from the refrigerator.

"I wasn't sure you were coming back," David said impatiently as I walked back into the shop.

As I hung my coat up, I said, "I didn't realize there was any rush."

"There you were wrong."

I looked around the shop, and there wasn't a single customer in sight. "I can see you're just overwhelmed with work."

"It's not that," David said. "Annie called a few minutes ago and said she wanted to talk. I hate to do this to you, but can I take the rest of the afternoon off?"

This could be trouble. "Did she say what she wanted to talk about?" I asked.

"No, why do you ask?"

"David, there's something you should

know before you meet her."

He narrowed his gaze. "Carolyn, what have you been up to?"

"What makes you ask me that?"

"Come on, I've known you my entire life. Spill."

There was no use denying it. "I had a talk with her an hour ago."

"You had no right," he said fiercely. "I swear, you're worse than my mother."

"High praise indeed," I said. "Don't you want to know what we talked about?"

"Do I even need to ask?" He had his hand on the door, but I had to stop him. David deserved to hear my suspicions, whether he wanted to or not.

"Move your hand, Carolyn." The calm resonance in his voice was a sure sign that he was angry.

"Not until you listen to what I have to say. I can be just as stubborn as you can be, you know that, don't you?"

He took a step back. "Talk."

"Do you know what happened to Annie's father?" I had to tread lightly here.

"Sure. He died pretty soon after she was born. Neither one of us had a dad growing up. It's something that's brought us close. What does that have to do with anything?"

"You know about the jewelry store robbery, don't you? The one where he was injured?"

He scratched his chin. "She mentioned it."

"It happened about the time your father left town," I said, not able to look into his eyes.

"So what? Wait a second. You can't be serious." I could hear his breathing become raspy. "You think my dad had something to do with it, don't you? Is that why you think he left town, because he was afraid of getting caught? You didn't even know him."

"Surely you don't think you did, David. He left before you were born, and you didn't see him again until the day he was murdered."

"He wasn't a crook. I don't believe it."

"I'm not saying he was, but think about it. If Annie held your father responsible for what happened to her dad, she could come after you, too."

"Carolyn, you've breathed in too many fumes from the kilns. I can't believe you're even suggesting this."

"I'm not saying it's true, but it's a possibility, and isn't that reason enough to be careful?"

"I'm leaving," he said. By the tone of his

voice, I knew better than to try to stop him again.

I probably shouldn't have said anything, not without more evidence than a gut feeling, but at least David would go to the rendezvous with his eyes open. At least I hoped he would. I felt guilty about accusing Annie, but if she had been involved with Richard Atkins's murder, David needed to be careful around her.

I knew I'd fret about David until I heard from him again, but after the way we'd left things, I didn't expect that would be anytime soon. In the meantime, I had more avenues to explore. Unlike our esteemed sheriff, I couldn't afford to focus on one suspect. Too many people had had reason to want Richard Atkins dead, and unfortunately, several of them were either friends or family of mine.

CHAPTER 12

I couldn't shut down Fire at Will again; I'd done that too many times in the past few months. The bottom line was starting to suffer, and I was never that far away from being in the red as it was. I didn't know many small stores that could afford to stay in business with the kind of hours I'd been keeping.

To my surprise, I had a few customers come in over the course of the rest of the afternoon, though none of them wanted to paint anything, or work with the raw clay in back, either. Still, by the time I closed out my register, I'd made enough to prove that staying open had been worthwhile, even if it did mean that I was no closer to solving Richard Atkins's murder.

I had locked up the shop and started for my car when I saw Kendra Williams and Rose Nygren huddled together in conversation in front of Hattie's Attic. I couldn't pass up a chance to listen in on two of my suspects colluding about something.

I tried to get close enough to hear what they were talking about, but their voices were too low for me to understand what they were saying.

"Hello, ladies," I said the second I realized that Kendra had spotted me approaching.

"Carolyn," Kendra said stiffly. Rose merely glared.

"What's going on?" I tried to keep a sunny and harmless expression on my face, though I doubted either one would buy it.

"None of your business," Rose said in an uncharacteristically harsh tone.

"Is that any way to talk to me? I've never done anything to you."

"Other than accuse me of murder?" Rose asked.

"I never accused you of anything. I've just been trying to find out what happened to Richard Atkins. Is that such a terrible thing to do?"

"That's why we have a police force," Kendra said.

"We both know that not much goes on in Maple Ridge that you don't know about," I said. "I'm sure the police could learn a thing or two about our fair town, if you chose to tell them."

Kendra shrugged, and I could tell she was weakening, but Rose said, "Don't let her flatter you. She just wants to know what we've been talking about."

Kendra nodded. "You're right. It's none of your concern, Carolyn."

"Fine, be that way," I said. "When Sheriff Hodges asks me about you two, I know just what I'll say."

Kendra snorted. "As if the sheriff would ever consult with you about anything."

"You see how often he comes by my shop," I said. "What do you think he's doing over there, asking for pottery tips?" Okay, that was a flat-out lie, but I didn't care. After all, the sheriff did spend an inordinate amount of time at Fire at Will, albeit only to scold me for my amateur sleuthing efforts.

Before Rose could dissuade her, Kendra said, "If you must know, we were discussing our alibis."

"Do you mean making them up?" I asked.

Rose snapped, "No, we were talking about whether we should step forward and tell the sheriff where we were the night of the murder, so he won't suspect us."

"You two were together?" I couldn't believe they hadn't told me sooner. Could it be true, or were they each covering for the other? Wait a second, what about Rose's glasses being left at the hospital? "But Rose, you were in the hospital waiting room three nights ago. I've already looked into that, and I've got your glasses to prove it."

"So you have been checking up on me," she said, the accusation thick in her voice.

"Are you telling me it's not true?"

"I took Edith Sampson there, but I couldn't wait the entire time for her. I had other things to do, so Kendra picked me up at the hospital, then dropped me off later so I could give Edith a ride home."

"Okay, that explains that, but then where exactly were you both the night of the murder?"

"In Burlington," Kendra said in triumph. "We were meeting with the new owners of our buildings."

"Wait a second, whoever bought your places owns mine, too. Why wasn't I told about this meeting?"

"I'm sure you got the same notice in the mail that we did, but since you were so busy with your investigation, you probably forgot all about it. Don't worry, we told the new management team all about you."

"I'll just bet you did," I said. If Kendra Williams was my character witness, I was already sunk. "What did they say?"

"Rents won't go up, at least not until the current agreements expire," Rose said. "We made sure of that. If you don't believe us, you can call them yourself."

"Do you have their number?" I asked.

"Are you seriously going to check our alibis?" Rose asked.

"I might, but I want to talk to these people myself. After all, they're going to be my landlords, too."

Kendra turned to Rose and said, "We might as well give her the number. She's going to find out sooner or later."

"Oh, go on, then."

Kendra nodded, then said, "I've got one of their cards. I'll be right back."

While she was inside, I turned to Rose and said, "You know, you could have saved me a lot of grief if you'd told me about this before."

"Why on earth were you under the impression it was my job to make your life easier?"

"You sound just like my uncle," I said. Taking a stab in the dark, I asked, "Are you two back together?"

"I told you before, we were never a couple in the first place." She hurried back to her shop, and when Kendra emerged a minute later, she looked around, then asked, "What did you do to Rose?"

"Nothing. She got tired of waiting and left," I said. "Is that for me?"

She nodded and handed me a business card. "Here, you can call them if you'd like."

"Kendra, I'm going to ask you the same thing I asked Rose. Why did you hint that you were on some mysterious tryst when I asked you about an alibi before? You made it sound as though you were with a man, not Rose."

"I don't approve of your snooping, and you know it. Besides, I thought if I spread a little rumor that I was seeing someone mysterious, it might make folks talk. I knew you'd never be able to keep it to yourself."

"As a matter of fact, I haven't told a soul," I said, then I walked toward my car.

Once inside my Intrigue, I pulled out my cell phone and called the management group. The secretary confirmed Rose and Kendra's alibi easily enough, and echoed the news that rents would stay the same as long as the current leases were in effect. That was something, anyway. I could strike two names off my list, and I felt positively giddy doing so. That just left Mayor Jenkins, my uncle, and Annie Gregg. At least the field was finally narrowing.

I'd just walked in the door at home when I

heard the telephone ring. "Hello?"

"You sound positively out of breath," Sandy said. "Did I catch you at a bad time?"

"No, I just got in. What's up?"

"I've been doing more digging into the ClayDate Corporation, and I found something I thought you'd like to know."

As I looked through the mail, which Bill had deposited on the counter, I said, "That's old news, Sandy."

"That's exactly what it's not," she said smugly.

"What do you mean?"

"ClayDate has been paying its business license fees every year, including this one. Does that sound like a defunct company to you?"

"No, it doesn't," I admitted. "Why would the mayor lie to me about it?"

"He's a politician, isn't he? It must be second nature for him. Doesn't that mean he and Richard were doing business more recently than he admitted?"

"It has to. Thanks, Sandy. I'm going to ask him about this the first chance I get."

"You're welcome," she said. "I'll keep rooting around."

"Do that," I said as I hung up. The mail was mostly bills and the rest was junk. Didn't anybody write real letters anymore?

I used to love getting mail. Of course, I hadn't written any letters myself for ages. I'd have to do that sometime soon if I expected to get any in return.

I walked back to Bill's workshop and noticed that the gopher had dug even more holes. I promised myself I'd look up gopher eradicators in the phone book after we ate dinner.

Bill wasn't in his shop. Where could he be? His truck was parked out front, and I hadn't seen any sign of him in the house. I hurried back inside, worried that something might have happened to him.

"Bill? Are you here?" No answer. I could feel the knot in my gut growing as I searched the house. Our bedroom was empty, and that just left the boys' old bedroom we'd converted into a guest room years before. If he wasn't in there, I'd call the sheriff.

At first I didn't see him, but as I flipped on the light, I breathed a sigh of relief. "Bill, what are you doing in here?"

"Didn't want to get in your way," he mumbled. "My hand was hurting, so I took a pill and went to bed. Turn off that light, will you?"

I did as he asked, then sat down on the edge of the bed. "Can I get you anything?"

"Just sleep," he said as he jammed a pillow over his head. I took the hint and left him alone.

There wasn't a thing in the world I could do for him, and I hated the feeling of helplessness. Since our two sons had moved away, Bill and I relied on each other for so much. Having him out of action left me feeling odd and uneasy.

Since it appeared that I would be dining alone tonight, I looked through the cabinets for something to eat. I couldn't face eggs again, and I hadn't yet shopped, so peanut butter and jelly would have to do. Except a layer of something was growing on top of the jelly, so that was out, too. Peanut butter sandwiches might be wonderful fare for a ten-year-old, but they didn't do much for me. I promised myself I'd go to the grocery store tomorrow. After eating my unfulfilling sandwich, I decided to pop some popcorn as a supplement. I wasn't in the mood for regular television, so I put *Casablanca* in the DVD player and settled in for a night with Bogart, Bergman, and friends.

Darkness dropped like a coin outside, and I shut off the lights in the den so I could enjoy the movie. But something started flickering on the television, and for a minute, I thought the set was going out. Then movement outside caught my eye, and

I paused the movie so I could get a better look. Someone was in our backyard with a flashlight! I peered out through the glass, but I couldn't see anything but a bobbing beam of light. Creeping into the guest room, I whispered, "Bill? Are you awake?"

No response but a snore.

"Bill?" This time my voice was louder, but it had no effect on his drug-induced slumber.

I could call the police. I should call the police. But first I wanted to see if I could catch a glimpse of who was out there.

Standing by the back door, I flipped on the back porch light, ready to catch whoever was out there, but the light didn't go on. The bulb must have burned out. It was going to be up to Sheriff Hodges to catch the interloper.

I got through to him on the telephone without too much trouble. "This is Carolyn Emerson. Somebody's creeping around outside my house with a flashlight."

"Have they tried to get in?"

"No. Right now, it looks like they're just standing there holding a flashlight."

"Can you see who it is?"

I peered into the darkness again, but I couldn't make out who the trespasser was. "I can't tell. Should I go outside for a better look?"

"No! Lock the doors and I'll be there in two minutes."

At least I'd managed to shake some of the rust off the sheriff. I didn't have any weapons in the house, but I did have a mop handle I could swing like a bat. I grabbed it and watched outside, waiting for something to happen. I had just about given up any hope of the sheriff coming when I saw another light and heard him shout, "Freeze."

The flashlight dropped and I heard running. My first thought was to go outside, but I decided it would be better to wait for the sheriff to come get me.

After the longest ten minutes of my life, I heard a tap on the back door, and I was so startled, I dropped the mop handle.

I could make out a man's shape, but I couldn't see his face. "Carolyn, let me in."

There was no mistaking the sheriff's voice. After I unlocked the door, he asked, "Where's Bill?"

"He's sleeping."

Hodges stared at me a few seconds, then asked, "You didn't think this was important enough to wake him?"

"He's on medication for his hand," I said. "Who was it?"

"I don't know," he admitted. "I lost him in the woods. I found this, though. Any chance it's yours?"

He reached back and collected a brand new shovel with dirt on its blade. "Are you kidding? I haven't bought a new yard tool in ten years. Where did you find it?"

"It was in the yard. It looks like your friend was digging holes. Any idea why?"

"I thought we had gophers," I said.

"Maybe the two-legged variety," he replied. "Why didn't you turn the back porch light on when I came up to the house? I could have been anybody."

"It must be burned out," I said. "Besides, I waited until I heard your voice before I let you in. What should I do now?"

"I'd get a new bulb if I were you."

"I'm not talking about the light. I mean the intruder."

"I doubt he's coming back tonight, but just in case, I'll have someone come by every hour or so to check on the place. If you don't mind, I'll keep this shovel."

"Be my guest," I said. Despite the problems I had with the sheriff, he had been prompt about coming out when I'd needed him. "Thanks for getting here so fast."

"It's part of my job," he said. "Don't forget to replace that bulb in the morning."

"I promise," I said.

Not even *Casablanca* could hold my attention after that. I popped the movie out of the DVD player, brushed my teeth, and decided to go to bed. The guest room was a single mattress, and there was no way Bill and I both would fit on it, at least not now that we were nearing our thirty-year anniversary. Not that I didn't love my husband — I probably loved him more after all our years together than I did the day I married him — but I wasn't willing to fight him all night for the covers on a bed two sizes too small.

Our bed seemed vast and empty without him, and I thought I'd never fall asleep, but the exhaustion from the day finally kicked in. I found myself drifting off as I wondered why on earth anyone would dig holes in our yard, at night to boot.

"I can't believe you slept through all of the excitement last night," I told my husband as he came into the kitchen for breakfast the next morning. I'd been up for hours and was dallying so I could see him before I had to leave to open the shop. Since Hannah and I were at odds, it meant we weren't meeting for coffee in the morning, and that left me with more free time than I liked.

"Why, what happened?" He was not nearly as fresh as he had been the day before. "Those pills really knocked me out."

"We had an intruder."

He sat up in his chair. "What?"

"Well, not in the house. Somebody was digging holes in the backyard last night with a flashlight."

"You can't dig much of a hole with one of those things," he said.

"He was using the flashlight to see, you nit," I said. "He had a shovel for digging. The sheriff took it with him."

"Hodges came out here? Why didn't you wake me?"

"I tried," I said, "but you were too far gone."

He walked over to the sink, took the bottle of pain pills, and tossed them in the trash.

"Why did you do that?"

"You needed me last night, and I was too doped up to help you. I don't need that kind of comfort."

I'd threatened to do the exact same thing myself, but now I had a change of heart. "Bill, don't be so rash. Everything was fine."

"But it might not have been," he said. "Why didn't you turn the porch light on and scare whoever it was away?"

"That's another thing. You need to put a

new bulb in the back porch light. That one's blown out."

"I changed it last week," he said.

"You don't have to do it right now," I said. "Eat your breakfast first."

"Just a second." He opened the back door and stepped outside. Twenty seconds later, he was back. "Flip the light on."

I did as he asked. "It's working perfect now," he said.

"Well, it wasn't last night."

He frowned. "The bulb was loose. I could have sworn I tightened it up all the way when I put it in."

I thought about that as I took a sip of coffee. "Maybe somebody unscrewed it."

"Now you're just being paranoid."

I pointed outside. "You said we had gophers, too."

He shrugged. "You made your point. I'll poke around a little after I eat."

"I'll go with you," I said.

"Don't you have a shop to run?"

I glanced at the clock. "I've got plenty of time. What would you like for breakfast?"

"I'm just going to have some orange juice."

As he poured a glass, I said, "You need to eat more than that."

"I'm not hungry. Those blasted pills kill

my appetite. That's enough reason to throw them away."

As he got dressed, I wondered again why anyone would invade our backyard. With the broad daylight to reassure me, I decided to go out and look around myself. Sure enough, I could see a clump of grass the digger had failed to replant. The hole was nearly six inches deep and twelve inches across. What could he have been looking for?

"What are you doing out here by yourself?" Bill said gruffly behind me.

"It's perfectly safe at the moment," I said. "What do you make of this?"

He peered down and studied the hole. "I may be wrong, but it looks like a hole to me."

"We've already established that," I said. "But why?"

"Hey, I answered a question. Now it's your turn."

"I don't have a clue," I said.

"Maybe you should get that shooting gang of yours to take a swing at it."

"They're called the Firing Squad, and you know it. I might just do that; it's not a bad idea."

"I was kidding, Carolyn."

"Well, I'm not." I glanced at my watch. "I

have to run. Try to stay out of trouble today, okay?"

"It's always my goal," he said, "but I'm not always that successful at it."

As I drove to Fire at Will, I continued to ask myself what the digging meant. Was there something back there worth excavating? I couldn't imagine what it might be. No pirates had ever made it to Maple Ridge, and as far as I knew, the closest gold strike had been hundreds of miles away. Something was out there, though. Or at least someone suspected there was.

I was surprised to find David in the shop when I arrived, a full half hour before he was due to punch in.

"You're here early," I said as I traded my jacket for an apron.

"I wanted to make up some of the time I've been missing lately," he admitted, a full-blown apology for David. "Our first batch of cottages is finished. Would you like to see them?"

"You bet," I said. He'd pulled them out of the kilns and lined them up on the table in back. They were unique, each beautiful in its own way. "It's like a tiny village."

"You read my mind. We should do snow-covered ones at Christmas. I bet we could make a fortune."

"That's a great idea," I said as I picked one up. "This is nice. You did a good job."

"Feel free to put it in the display window. You're welcome to get what you can for it."

I frowned at him. "I thought this was for Annie."

"It was, but I'm afraid she'd just throw it at me if I tried to give it to her."

"I thought you two had patched up your differences," I said.

"So had I. Evidently, I was wrong. I don't want to talk about it, if it's okay with you."

"That's fine," I said. David had a right to his privacy; I quickly turned the discussion back to the cottages. "We could do a winter display now. I've got some spun fiber from last year."

"Not with summer almost here, but we should do something with them. Let's see what we can come up with."

We tried a dozen different layouts in the front window before we came up with something we both agreed on. I walked out onto the street to get a better look at it from the customer's perspective. As I stood there assessing our efforts, I heard someone calling me from the street.

I turned around to see Mayor Jenkins sitting in a brand new car. "Carolyn, do you have a minute?"

"I suppose," I said. "What can I do for you?"

He eased the passenger-side door open. "Why don't you get in so we can talk?"

I saw something in his eyes that I didn't like.

I said firmly, "No thanks. I'm fine out here."

"Carolyn, I don't want to have to crane my neck to look at you. Come on. Get in." That was more of an order than a request, and I didn't obey commands very well.

"I don't think so. You can get out, if you want to."

He did just that, slamming the door. "You're a stubborn woman, you know that?"

"I like to think of myself as independent," I said. "What did you want to talk about?"

"This snooping you're doing. It needs to stop, and I mean now."

"Harvey, were you under the impression you were my boss? I don't take orders from anybody; not my husband, and certainly not you."

"Maybe you should reconsider that policy," he said.

"And perhaps you should tell the truth when someone asks you a question."

He scowled. "What are you talking about?"

"ClayDate. I found out it's not old news after all. You've been renewing it every year, and I know you, Harvey. You wouldn't spend a penny on it if that business weren't still active."

"You don't know what you're talking about," he said. "There's a lot more to me than you realize."

Why was he being so defensive? "Prove me wrong. I'm willing to listen to what you have to say."

"Carolyn, what I do or don't do is none of your business."

"Is it really worth having me on your case about this for the next month or two? You know I won't back off until I know the truth. Come clean with me, Harvey."

He shook his head, then spat out his next words. "Fine. If it will shut you up, I'll tell you. I made a promise a long time ago to a man who did me a favor when he didn't have to, and I'm enough of a blamed fool to keep it. As long as I'm drawing breath, Clay-Date will stay in business. It's as simple as that. Now, are you satisfied?"

"Not really. There's got to be more to it than that."

He snorted. "That's your problem, not mine. You're never content, even when you get the truth." He stopped and stared at me a second before adding, "Remember what I said about nosing around things that aren't any of your business."

"It's etched in my mind forever," I replied with a smile. "Don't think for a minute that it will alter my behavior in any way, though."

He shook his head, got in the car, and drove off.

David had been watching openly from the window. "What was that all about?"

"I don't think the mayor wants my vote during the next election."

"It didn't look like it, did it? What did he say, Carolyn?"

I thought about shrugging him off, but David had a right to know. We worked together, and he was more than just an assistant to me, he was like another son. "He told me to quit snooping." I wasn't about to get into the mayor's rationale for keeping an old corporation in business long past its earning potential for him. Was it really as simple as that? Was ClayDate still viable because of a promise he made long ago? I couldn't be sure. Men baffled me sometimes. I've seen sterner and harder men than the mayor do things for sentimental reasons that would make a schoolgirl blush. Maybe he was telling the truth.

David wasn't about to let up. "He was

more specific than that. You've been stirring up a dozen different pots, haven't you?"

"At least. I don't want to talk about that right now. We need to work on our display some more. Are you sure you don't want to keep the cottage you made for Annie? It might make a nice apology."

"Thanks, but I'll pass. I'm tired of saying I'm sorry. I don't even know what I'm apologizing for at this point."

I kept my mouth shut, something that would surprise Bill, if he knew about it.

We opened Fire at Will, and to my surprise and delight, by the time our lunch hours rolled around, we'd sold three cottages, with four more on order. "Can you believe how these are selling?" I said as I added our last one to the display.

"I've got a feeling I'm going to be making more of them."

I patted his shoulder. "Look at it this way. You get to work in clay, and that can't be all bad."

"I don't want to mass-produce anything."

"I don't want that either, David. Make them all unique. Give them your special touch. And add a cat to one every now and then, though, would you?"

"I don't do requests," he said, his smile softening his words.

"Come on, that's usually all we do around here. If you don't want to add any cats to yours, I'll make a few and add them to mine. I think making these cottages is fun."

"I guess," he said. "Do you want to take your lunch break first, or should I?"

"You go ahead," I said. "I want to finish up a few of these."

David had been gone ten minutes when the front door chimed. It was my uncle, and I could tell from the scowl on his face that he was not at all happy with his only niece. Yet again.

CHAPTER 13

"Why do I get the feeling you're not here on a social call," I said.

"Maybe you're smarter than you look after all, but I sincerely doubt it."

"You always were a charmer. What's wrong now?"

"You."

"That encompasses a lot of ground. Could you be more specific than that?"

Don Rutledge frowned as he looked around my shop. "Butting into other people's lives is bad for business, and it's going to be bad for you."

"Are you threatening me?" Here was my own flesh and blood, standing in my shop trying to intimidate me. Sadly, it was working.

"I'm trying to help you," he said. "Don't you get it?"

"Apparently not. How is your blustering supposed to do me any good?"

"Carolyn, life is not just one big game. This is serious business."

"I never said it wasn't, but that doesn't mean I've got to stop digging. Speaking of which, do you mind if I look at your hands?"

"My hands? What has that got to do with anything? Have you completely lost your mind?"

"Probably. Let me see them." I'd made it a point to look at the mayor's hands when we'd had our tête-à-tête earlier; they'd been clean and without calluses or blisters. So had the sheriff's the night before. Okay, I hadn't really suspected him of digging up my backyard, but I'd looked all the same.

My uncle, shaking his head in obvious disbelief, held out both hands. They were tough and calloused, and bits of dirt embedded around his nails made it clear that he was used to working in his own garden soil. "What's this about?"

"Just checking," I said.

"What, are you on cuticle patrol now? Stay out of this, Carolyn."

When was everyone going to stop trying to tell me what to do? "Fine," I said, just to get him off my back.

"I don't believe you," he said.

"I can't do anything about that, now can I?"

My uncle stared at me a few seconds, then left the shop. I was aggravating a great many people lately, and I didn't envy the sheriff his task if someone decided to get rid of me. The suspects would be too numerous to name.

Just then Butch walked into the shop. "Those are new, aren't they?"

"Are you talking about the cottages?"

"Yeah. I'd like to try my hand at one of those sometime. Are they hard?"

"Not for you. Why don't you grab an apron and we can make one together right now?"

He glanced at his watch. "Sorry, but I'm running behind as it is. I just thought you might like to know something I just found out."

"You bet. At the moment, I'm at a complete loss."

Butch looked around the shop. "You don't have to keep after this, you know."

"Why does everyone keep telling me that? I need help, not discouragement." I was becoming increasingly exasperated with people. They could either lend a hand, or get out of my way. There wasn't room for any other option.

"That's why I'm here. I've been asking around about what really happened twenty years ago, and I may have finally gotten the right guy to talk."

"You didn't do anything drastic, did you?" I was in constant fear that Butch would slide back into a life of crime, and I certainly didn't want to do anything to encourage that kind of behavior. Then again, it was a little hypocritical of me to take so freely the information he offered.

"No, this guy was thrilled to have somebody in the business to talk to. We don't exactly form social clubs when we retire, you know what I mean? Anyway, this fella used to be a fence in Marston, and he handled some of the jewels from the robbery that happened in Maple Ridge about the time Richard disappeared."

"Just some of the merchandise? How can he possibly remember that after all these years?"

"The man could tell you every piece he's ever touched. He's like a baseball nut who can recite the batting averages for every player in the 1958 World Series, you know?"

"I don't suppose he gave you the name of the thief, did he? Or is that a question of honor among thieves?"

Butch laughed. "You've been watching too much television. As far as I've seen, that bunk is just that, pure hogwash. No, my friend didn't cooperate that much, but he did say that some of the best pieces weren't offered to him for sale. He only handled a few items, so he started to wonder how many partners had held the place up. Evidently there were some onyx brooches, a handful of gold rings, and lots of diamonds that never turned up. When my friend asked the guy about the things that were missing, the guy said that the rest of his share was someplace safe, stashed away where nobody would ever find it but him, and then he added something odd. He said that it was in the pits and kind of chuckled something about poetic justice. Kind of a crazy comment to make, wouldn't you say? It's not typical behavior for a crook."

"I didn't think there was such a thing as typical behavior," I said.

Butch laughed. "You've got a point. Listen, I've got to run. Call me if you need me."

"I will. And Butch? I'm sorry I snapped at you earlier."

"Hey, you're entitled to unload now and then. I'm a big boy; I can take it." He shot me with his finger as he left, and for some reason, the gesture made me smile.

When David came back from lunch, he asked, "What's up, Carolyn? You've got the oddest expression on your face."

"Do you know what it's like when you've seen or heard something that you know is significant, but you don't know how?"

"It happens," he admitted.

"So, what do you do to figure it out?"

David thought about it a few seconds, then said, "I always try not to think about it. Do something else, put it out of your mind, and it will come to you."

"Like not thinking of blue elephants, right?" I asked.

"What? Did I miss something?"

"It's an old parlor game. For the next thirty seconds, you can think of anything in the world. Just not blue elephants. Ready? Go."

I stopped him three seconds later. "Quick, what were just thinking about?"

"Blue elephants," he reluctantly admitted. "Why don't you try having lunch, then? That might jar something loose."

"It might, but even if it doesn't, I still get to eat, so there's no real downside, is there?"

I left the shop, but instead of going to Shelly's or In the Grounds, I decided to swing by the grocery store and pick up some things for a proper lunch with my husband. I'd fed him an omelet the day before, but today I pulled out all the stops. I grabbed some roast beef and provolone cheese from the deli, along with some crisp French bread, and on a whim, I added a bottle of wine to my basket. Bill and I were going to dine in style.

I drove home, trying not to think about holes, or blue elephants, for that matter, but I didn't have much luck.

Bill wasn't in the house — I even checked in the guest bedroom — which meant he had to be in his shop. I put everything out on the counter and stared out the window as I started making our sandwiches.

Then it hit me. I knew what the fence had really told Butch, and why someone was digging in our backyard. It all came together, as if a jigsaw puzzle had just fallen from the sky and landed in perfect alignment.

Leaving everything where it was, I rushed to our garage, grabbed an old, rusted shovel, and headed into the yard. If I was right, I might just have the answer to all my questions. And if I was wrong, we'd have one more hole in the yard.

I didn't think I was wrong, though. The sandy indentation had been there twenty-five years, first as a horseshoe-throwing pit, and then as a cooling area for my pottery. The missing jewelry was literally in the pits.

It had to be. I wedged the shovel into the ground around the perimeter of the sandy area, searching for any sign that I was right. The digging was hard, since we hadn't had much rain lately, and I was beginng to fear I wasn't going to be able to go deep enough when my blade hit something between the edge of the pit and the gas kiln.

It was a pot, but not one I'd ever made. I moved as much dirt as I could with my hands and finally uncovered a small, earthen pot buried deep in the soil. Something was inside it, and as I hefted it out of the hole, the pot cracked open, most likely as a result of that first blow from my shovel. Inside, I could see a dirt-covered box.

This had to be what my backyard digger had been looking for! My hands were shaking as I worked the box free from the remains of the clay container. Despite the dirt, I could tell it was from the jewelry store robbery so long ago.

That's when I heard a voice behind me say, "Good job, Carolyn. I knew you could do it, if I gave you enough time to look." My blood chilled in my veins as I realized my uncle had been behind it all from the very start. I couldn't believe someone close to me, a member of my own family, could be capable of the things he must have done, but the proof was pretty clear. If I was going to survive this confrontation, I had to come up with a way to stop him before he hurt anybody else, including me.

My right hand started drifting toward the shovel, but I felt a foot crash down on my fingers. I yelled out in pain.

"Not so fast. I don't want you getting any ideas. I've got your husband tied up in his shop, and if you do as you're told, you'll both walk away from this alive. Let's go; he's waiting for us."

I knew the threat was real. If I didn't do something quickly, I was sure Bill and I would soon be dead.

I turned slowly, and Don ordered, "Bring the box with you. You just couldn't let it go, could you? Curiosity might end up killing more than just the cat."

My flesh crawled at the sound of his words. Dutifully, I grabbed the box, wondering if I could use it as some kind of weapon. The edges had sharp corners, but I'd have to move quickly and decisively at just the right time, or I'd only anger the killer more.

He said, "Nice and easy. That's right. Let's go over to the workshop, shall we?"

I knew that once we were inside, Don would be able to deal with us easily. If I could keep him outside, there was a chance that one of my neighbors would see us and get suspicious. It was worth a shot, anyway.

"I knew it had to be you," I said as I turned to my uncle and looked him straight in the eye. He had a handgun pointed at me, partially concealed by a folded towel, but it was clear enough to me what it was.

"Don't try to tell me that," Don said. "I was careful not to leave any clues behind."

"They're everywhere, if you just know where to look."

"Go on, I'm listening."

"Let's take that ring for starters. It's from the robbery, isn't it? That was careless of you to keep wearing it, because it matches the general description of one that was taken," I said, recalling what Butch had told me.

He glanced at it, then said, "It suited me. Besides, everyone who knew that it was part of the haul was either dead or gone. To be honest with you, I nearly forgot where I'd gotten it. You've got to have more than that."

"You were too quick to unload on me the first time I talked to you," I said. "That was a red flag from the start. When I came out to see you after the murder, you didn't lower that gun barrel until you found out that I was looking for information and not there to accuse you of murder. What happened, Don, did your guilty conscience get the best of you?"

"Why would you think I would kill him after all these years? Rose got over it. So did I."

"It wasn't about Rose at all," I said. Where was everybody? Normally I couldn't take out the trash or go get the newspaper without someone butting into my business, but now a man was threatening me with a gun in broad daylight, and no one was around. "You were looking for this box from the start. Richard was blackmailing you with what's inside it, wasn't he? Don't bother denying it, it's the only thing that makes sense. Were you two partners in the robbery?"

My uncle laughed coarsely. "What's it going to hurt to tell you now? Do you think I'd be stupid enough to be partners with him? I committed the robbery myself. It was just dumb luck that he saw me coming out of the store that night and demanded a split of the take. I thought about killing him then, too, but he was too smart for me."

"So that's why you've been digging in my backyard the last few nights. Did you follow him here the first night he was back in town?"

Don nodded. "I saw him leaving your

shop and followed him the rest of the day. I knew he had to have come back to Maple Ridge to check up on his stash. Richard wouldn't tell me where the box was when I confronted him that night, and I lost my temper. He was going to dig it up. I knew it had to be somewhere around here, but I wasn't having much luck on my own. It was nice of you to dig it up for me."

"So the rest of it was just a smokescreen," I said. "Seeing David, the lecture, all of it."

"It was enough to fool Hodges. That's all of the questions I'm going to answer. Let's go back to Bill's workshop where we can talk about this without your neighbors around. Go on, Carolyn, and don't get any funny ideas."

"There's nothing remotely humorous about all of this," I said.

Poor Bill. Was he already dead? It was clear that my uncle was capable of murder. If he'd killed my husband, I'd find a way to stay alive long enough to make him pay for it.

"Go on inside." He nudged me with the gun when I hesitated at the doorway.

I walked in expecting the worst, but relief flooded through me when I saw that Bill was still alive. Don had bound him to a chair and had taped his mouth, but I could still see Bill's eyes. He was trying to tell me something, I knew it, but I couldn't figure out what it was. As my uncle started to raise the gun, I said, "There's nothing in the box. You know that, don't you? It's too light."

"You're bluffing." A worried expression crossed his face, though I knew it would pass when he felt the weighty box.

"See for yourself." I started to offer it to him when there was a noise behind us. Bill had somehow managed to free himself, at least one arm. He ripped the tape off his mouth and screamed ferociously, like a wild animal attacking.

Don's aim shifted from me to my husband, and I hit his gun arm as hard as I could with a sharp corner of the box. A shiver went through me as I struck him, a physical memory of defending myself once before.

He dropped the gun and yelped in pain. That was all the opening I needed. As he knelt down to retrieve the weapon, I grabbed a length of oak Bill had turned on a lathe and shaped like a baseball bat, and I struck Don in the back with everything I had.

My uncle hit the floor hard, like a bag of dirt.

I started for Bill when he shouted, "Get

his gun first."

"He's not coming around anytime soon," I said.

"Just do it, Carolyn," he commanded, and I obeyed. I took the gun, and stared down at my uncle. Had I killed him with the force of that blow? If I had, I promised myself I wouldn't let it destroy me. The man was a cold-blooded killer, and he deserved what he got, even if he was my kin.

As I started to untie Bill, he said, "Get that knife on the bench and cut me free."

"These ropes are expensive," I said. "Give me a second. I'll get it."

"Carolyn, don't push our luck."

I gave up on the knot and grabbed the knife. "Don't move," I said.

As soon as he was free, he leapt to his feet and threw his arms around me. "I didn't think you'd get my signal."

"What signal? I could see you were trying to tell me something, but I couldn't for the life of me figure out what it was."

"I was gesturing to my back," he said plaintively. "I managed to free one arm while he was out there with you, and I was working on the other one when you showed up." He cradled his cut hand against his chest. "I wish I hadn't thrown those pills away."

"Don't worry, we can get you more." My hand was throbbing from the stomp Don had given it, and I might need a pill myself to get to sleep that night.

Bill shook his head, and I could see he was shaking. "That was too close. I can't believe how hard you hit him."

I couldn't believe it myself. The adrenaline that had been shooting through me was nearly gone, and I felt my knees weaken. "We're safe now; that's all that counts."

"Thanks for saving me," he said in a humbled voice. "I've never felt so helpless in my life."

I tapped him lightly under the chin. "You saved us both, you old fool. If you hadn't worked your arm free and taken that tape off, you never would have been able to distract him like that. Nice yell, by the way. You managed to rattle me, too."

"So I guess we saved each other," he said.

"I like that," I agreed. "There's a certain symmetry to it, isn't there? Would you like to call Sheriff Hodges, or should I?"

"I'll let you have the privilege." He looked down at Don and shook his head. "So, it was all for nothing. The box was empty."

"Hardly," I said as I started to open it. My hands were shaking as I worked the clasp free and lifted the lid. As I gazed inside, I asked, "I wonder if there's a finder's fee for this? There's a necklace in here that I absolutely adore."

"If there's not a reward, I'll buy it for you out of my woodworking money."

"That's all right," I said as I closed the lid. "It's probably too fancy for me anyway."

I heard Don groan, and despite what I'd vowed earlier, I was glad I hadn't killed him.

"You watch him while I go make that call," I said.

Bill picked up the turned piece of wood. "Go on, but hurry. I don't like playing guard duty."

"If he somehow manages to get up after the way I hit him, you should be able to glare at him hard enough to drop him again."

Chapter 14

The next day, I was working at Fire at Will when the sheriff came in.

"I just wanted to let you know that your uncle confessed to the murder."

"Don't call him that," I said. "He stopped being family a long time ago."

He shrugged. "I don't blame you a bit for feeling that way. Are we good?"

I looked at him, thought of about a thousand things I could say, but surprised myself by answering, "Never better."

"Sometimes worse though, right?" Was that a smile I saw on his lips? It happened so briefly I couldn't be sure.

After the sheriff left, the older gentleman returned for his sister's cottage, and I had it ready and waiting for him. As he paid the bill, he said, "I couldn't help noticing your front window."

I smiled. "In a way, it's all your fault. I enjoyed making those cottages so much, I kind of got carried away. What can I say? You inspired me."

"It's a nice scene. Most of us spend our lives trying to go home again, don't we?"

I smiled. "I don't know; I'm kind of happy the way things are right here and now."

He saluted me with two fingers as he made his way to the door. "Then you are a truly lucky woman."

"You don't have to tell me that," I said as he walked out with a smile on his face.

Twenty minutes later, three people I never expected to see together came into the shop, practically arm in arm. Hannah, David, and Annie looked as though they'd found a way to come to grips with their situation.

Hannah said, "We need to talk to you, but I get to go first." She smiled at the kids, and added, "I won the coin toss."

"I wanted to go two out of three," David chimed in.

"Let your mother talk," Annie corrected him, and to my amazement, David did just as she'd asked.

"Carolyn, anybody can say what their friends want to hear, but it takes someone special to point out something that might be tough to take. Thank you."

"You're welcome," I said. "But I'm disappointed in one thing."

"What's that?" She looked alarmed, so I decided I'd better stop toying with her.

"You don't have any presents with you."

"I'm taking care of that," Annie said. She came forward and hugged me. "Thank you for finding my father's jewelry."

"I imagine you have to give it back to the insurance company," I said. "That's a real shame."

"They never paid his claim," Annie said brightly. "Everything you found belongs to me. Do you know what that means? When I sell the jewelry, I'll be able to finally go to Stanford. It will be all mine as soon as the case is settled. I'm so happy."

"There wasn't that much in there, was there?" I knew the costs to go to such a fine school were astronomical.

"You'd be surprised. But don't forget, I've been saving for years. I was getting close, but the jewelry will put me over the top. I want you to have something."

She reached into her bag and brought out a brightly wrapped present.

"I can't accept that," I said.

"I insist," she said.

Well, it wouldn't hurt to unwrap it. Instead of the necklace, there was a nice ring with a diamond that, while not huge, was still substantial.

"Thanks," I said, "but I meant it. I can't accept it." She started to frown when I added, "Think of it as a small scholarship. There's just one condition, though."

"What's that?"

"You have to promise not to use the money from its sale on anything practical. Set up a fund for pizza runs and ice cream parties. There's more to school, and life, than working all the time."

She nodded, and I could see tears tracking down her cheeks.

"Are you crying?" David asked her.

"Of course not," she mumbled. "Restroom?"

I pointed to the back, and she ducked in to repair her makeup.

David said, "I never understood why women cry when they're happy. She was happy, wasn't she?"

"David, what am I going to do with you?" Hannah asked.

"He's too old to throw back, so I guess you're going to have to keep him," I said.

We laughed, and David scowled slightly. All was well with the world again.

Annie came out and gave me a hug. "Thank you."

"Just do as I ask, and I'll be happy."

"I promise," she said. "David, are you ready?"

"Let's go." He turned to me and said, "We're driving to Boston to talk to some jewelry appraisers and find one who'll give top dollar for what you found. You two don't want to come, do you?"

It was clear from his expression that our company was the last thing in the world he wanted.

"Sorry, I've got to keep the shop open."

"And I have a class to teach," Hannah added.

They were gone before we could blink.

Hannah said, "It's nice they asked. So, you don't get a present after all."

"You're back in my life. That's the only gift I need," I said. "I'm sorry I was so abrupt with you."

"You were brutal," she acknowledged. "But I needed it. I'm going to try to step back a little. I may need some help."

"Don't worry, if your apron strings start to constrict, I'll step in and say something."

"I know I can count on you. Do you really need to keep the shop open?"

"Why, don't you have a class to teach?"

"My TA can handle it. After all, that's what teacher's assistants are for."

"I'm game if you are," I said. "What did

you have in mind?"

"Nothing as exciting as a trip to Boston, but I was thinking a nice long coffee break might be in order."

"Lead the way," I said. As I locked the shop up, I glanced at the store window. Our cottages were lined up like a village street, making me think of our quaint little town. Maple Ridge was a wonderful place to live, but it wasn't perfect. Greed could have dire consequences. Richard Atkins's greed had gotten him killed, and my uncle's had nearly ended my life — and my husband's — all for a few cold, hard stones.

And unlike pliable clay that could be reworked and used again, Richard's and Don's lives were destroyed forever, like fired porcelain that was shattered beyond all hope of repair.

I chose to look at it positively, though. Annie had her education paid for, David had his life ahead of him, and I had my best friend Hannah and my husband, Bill, as well as two bright and healthy sons.

It was more than most folks had, and for me, it was everything I needed.

CLAY-CRAFTING TIPS
WEAVING CLAY

There's a real artistry in weaving clay. If you have access to a kiln, you can weave potter's clay, but don't despair if all you have is modeling clay. Many brands can be used to form a nice woven basket that you can temper in your oven. Be sure to read the package's instructions before starting your project.

As Carolyn demonstrated to the Firing Squad, knead your clay and then roll it into a flat sheet the thickness you want. If you're using modeling clay, you can dress up your creation by using different colors of clay. After you've rolled out the clay to a quarter-inch thickness, cut it into uniform strips. I like to make mine around an inch wide, but you don't have to be exact. Lay out half the strips side by side vertically, and then take one of the remaining strips and weave it horizontally in and out of the vertical strips, going over one and then under the next.

Repeat until you've used all but four of the remaining strips.

After you've completed the pattern, you should have a woven square. Now comes the fun part. Using a bone or a rib, bend the four corners up until you have a bowl shape. You can squeeze and pinch the clay at this stage to get the shape you desire. To dress the edges after you're done, take the final four strips of the clay and bend them lengthwise over the rough edges of the basket. Then bake your bowl per the directions on the clay package.

And as always, the most important thing to remember is to have fun! If you're not happy with the results before you fire the clay, knead it all together again and start over. That's one of the beauties of working with clay.

We hope you have enjoyed this Large Print book. Other Thorndike, Wheeler, and Chivers Press Large Print books are available at your library or directly from the publishers.

For information about current and upcoming titles, please call or write, without obligation, to:

Publisher
Thorndike Press
295 Kennedy Memorial Drive
Waterville, ME 04901
Tel. (800) 223-1244

or visit our Web site at:

http://gale.cengage.com/thorndike

OR

Chivers Large Print
published by BBC Audiobooks Ltd
St James House, The Square
Lower Bristol Road
Bath BA2 3SB
England
Tel. +44(0) 800 136919
email: bbcaudiobooks@bbc.co.uk
www.bbcaudiobooks.co.uk

All our Large Print titles are designed for easy reading, and all our books are made to last.